STAND-OFF AT BLUE STACK

Two gunmen walk into Tucson Joel Cramer's soddy, murder his wife and snatch his young son. Cramer sets out to find his boy, but instead crosses the crooked Marshal Butch Farrall and rides into a web of corruption. With gambler Jak La Roche at his side, Cramer meets the evil half-breed Dyke Manson, settles with both of the killers, only to be told that his son has been taken by Quanah Parker's renegade Comanche. It would all end in a bloody showdown at Blue Stack.

Books by Will Keen
in the Linford Western Library:

HIGH PLAINS SHOWDOWN

WILL KEEN

STAND-OFF AT BLUE STACK

Complete and Unabridged

LINFORD
Leicester

First published in Great Britain in 2000 by
Robert Hale Limited
London

First Linford Edition
published 2001
by arrangement with
Robert Hale Limited
London

British Library CIP Data

Keen, Will
   Stand-off at Blue Stack.—Large print ed.—
Linford western library
   1. Western stories
   2. Large type books
   I. Title
   823.9′14 [F]

   ISBN 0–7089–9735–X

Published by
F. A. Thorpe (Publishing)
Anstey, Leicestershire

Set by Words & Graphics Ltd.
Anstey, Leicestershire
Printed and bound in Great Britain by
T. J. International Ltd., Padstow, Cornwall

This book is printed on acid-free paper

1

They came into Joel Cramer's soddy out of a rain-swept Kansas night, walking into the single room with a rattle of the latch and a whisper of oiled hinges, dripping water onto the packed earth floor from shiny yellow slickers and bringing with them the smell of darkness and fear. Two of them, their stovepipe boots caked with mud, the lower halves of their faces masked by filthy bandannas knotted under ragged unwashed hair that poked from beneath rain-sodden felt hats whose brims sagged heavily over cruel, glittering eyes.

The cold wet wind gusted in after them, bending the flames of the oil lamps so that their dim light cast giant, moving shadows that drew the small boy's wide brown eyes.

Then the one with the greasy blond

hair and ice-blue eyes cocked his shotgun. He made a big show of it, easing the two hammers back with the heel of his thumb until they clicked; and he made sure that while he snapped those hammers back the twin blued muzzles never wavered, remaining always lined up on the woman's faded shift dress and the clear restless outline of her firm breasts.

The boy gurgled in delight, turning his tow-head to watch as the gun barrel flashed and among the shadows highlights danced.

'Oh, God,' Fran Cramer said softly, and in a swift movement she bent to gather him into her arms, lifting him from his tiny wooden chair set close to the comforting heat of the iron wood-burner, her own eyes wide now, huge and luminous and fearful in her suddenly ashen face.

'Weren't you here a fortnight back with Manson,' Joel Cramer said, 'warning me off Jackson's Creek? Ain't he man enough to do his own dirty work?' He came to his feet, knocking the edge of the heavy pine table with his thighs so that the supper dishes rattled.

The questions went unanswered. The blue-eyed man with the shotgun spat wetly on the floor.

'You,' he rasped at the woman. 'Hand over the boy.'

'Wha . . . ?' Her hands fluttered as she hugged the child. She turned her head jerkily in her panic, her eyes wild. 'Joel, help me, I — '

Boots scraped as the second man moved forward into the shifting circle of yellow light. A small circle on the dirty bandanna was moist, billowing in and out as he breathed through his mouth. Beneath tangled black eyebrows one milk-white eye was canted sideways in a knife-ruined socket. He fixed the other on Joel Cramer, said in his harsh, grating voice, 'You want to help her, you tell her to do just what the man says.'

'Hand over our son, Johnny, to a

couple of Manson's killers?'

'To me. *Pronto*.'

Without waiting he took a fast stride towards Fran Cramer and the slicker rustled and sprayed glittering droplets as his hands were thrust out and his thick fingers reached for the boy's waist.

'You leave him alone, you — !'

The blast of the shotgun was a huge charge of dynamite in the enclosed room, the muzzle-flame like sheet lightning in its brilliance. Rank moist earth and twisted roots showered down from the roof. A spider scuttled into the shadows. The woman screamed. Shock drove her backwards against the wall where the old Henry repeater hung, the impact slackening her hold on the child. A framed tintype slid with a whisper of sound and the brittle crack of glass. In that instant the boy, now squealing with fright, was gone, torn from her slack grasp and borne swiftly towards the door.

'Johnny!'

Fran Cramer's scream turned into a shriek that rose to the brink of hysteria and was instantly choked off. What emerged then was a muffled wail of anguish that brought Joel Cramer to the brink of tears as his wife pressed white knuckles to her teeth and bit down hard.

Cramer came around the table in a rush, the shotgun's blast ringing in his ears, the silent menace of the second charged barrel forgotten. A chair clattered over, was kicked away. His blazing eyes ignored the armed man with the smoking scattergun, instead peering anxiously towards the open door through which fine wind-driven rain drifted like a glistening mist.

He was brought up short, stopping as if he had run into one of the soddy's two-foot thick walls as the man with the ice-blue eyes pulled the second trigger.

The thunderous blast brought Cramer

swinging around so fast he over-balanced and fell hard against the table. His glance noted the angle of the shotgun. His head snapped round and he stared in horror at the front of his wife's shift dress. It was torn to shreds by the charge of lead shot that had ripped into her soft body at close range, already soaked with slick red blood.

The Henry she had dragged from its wall hooks fell from her hand to hit the floor with a clatter.

Cramer said something, but the memory of the words — if words they were — was forever lost. An arm came up, not in fury but in a blind reaction, the simple unconscious act of pushing the killer out of the way so that he could get past to reach the woman he loved and hold her in his arms as she died.

Then the empty shotgun came around in a vicious, back-handed swing. The twin barrels cracked against Joel Cramer's forehead and suddenly he was wallowing in deep black water, floating forwards with hands outstretched as he blindly sought a cold river-bed that was out of sight and out of reach and eluded him until he knew no more . . .

2

Fran's dried blood covered most of the front of Joel Cramer's shirt. A dark, ugly patch exposed by the cold light of a late spring dawn, it stiffened the cloth and scratched against his skin as the night's dying wind flattened the garment against his chest and he moved in the saddle to the big horse's regular gait.

As he crossed the flat emptiness of the Kansas prairie on the ten mile ride to Jackson's Bend, it had not yet occurred to Cramer that he would resolve to wear that shirt until he did the only thing he could for his wife now that she was gone: find her boy and bring him home.

Nor had it occurred to him that he might find that task beyond his capabilities, and that mental lapse was something for which he could be thankful. With his mind still tortured by horrific images of cold-blooded murder and a screaming child being carried away into the dark night, thoughts of failure added to those of cowardice might easily have driven him over the edge.

He knew that he had come close to snapping in those cold hours before dawn when the human soul is at its lowest ebb. Standing on the storm-swept ridge against which he had erected the soddy, with the fitful moonlight gleaming on the shifting grasslands and the dark wet earth of Fran's grave, he had reached just about the lowest point in his whole life. It had taken a powerful effort of will to throw down the shovel, turn his back on the simple wooden cross and walk away; scarcely any effort at all to take the drum of coal oil and a flaming brand to their home of six short weeks and watch through his tears and the rolling black smoke as the contents of the soddy burned, for without her and the boy he was alone and would have been unable to bear its emptiness.

What thinking he did allow himself on that ride into town was measured, and calculating. In the past weeks he had feared a visit from a renegade band of Quanah Parker's Comanches, rumoured to have moved up from the Texas Panhandle, crossed Indian Territory into Kansas and established a camp somewhere on Jackson's Creek. But in the dying seconds of Fran's life, in that brief time that was measurable in missed heartbeats and opportunities and the shrill squeals of a frightened child, he had asked the blond killer if they were from Manson, and everything that had happened since had convinced him that he had guessed right.

So now, sitting in front of the desk in the marshal's office in the town of Jackson's Bend, he said, 'I want you to ride with me to Dyke Manson's place.'

The man behind the desk might have been hewn from the same crude stock as Jackson's Bend, travelled down the same bleak road to arrive at the ruin and despair that was evident in the town and his cluttered office. He was fat and filthy, a dark-haired man with thick stubble covering the lower half of a greasy face. The ash from the mangled cheroot dangling from his wet lips dusted the front of his unwashed shirt and settled like white dust on the tarnished badge of office. His thick-fingered hands, the nails black and chipped, rested on the desk and toyed with a Stetson that was ragged and misshapen and encrusted with dried sweat.

But the black eyes buried in the pouched flesh beneath his heavy brows were bright as buttons, and had been studying Cramer from the moment he walked in through the open door and dropped into the creaking wooden chair.

'This got anything to do with that mess of blood soaking your shirt — or did that come about when you cut yourself shaving?'

11

His fat belly wobbled against the desk as he chuckled deep in his throat at his own crude humour. Ash fell from the dead cheroot, and as the laugh turned into a choking cough he plucked it from of his mouth and mashed it into a brass ashtray.

'Two of Manson's hands used a shotgun to kill my wife,' Cramer said, 'then kidnapped my son. I want them arrested, then hanged.'

'Any witnesses?'

'Me. I'll ride with you, identify them.'

'Ain't good enough. You sure you ain't got confused between them and Comanche Injuns?'

In the tense silence, the marshal's breath rasped in his throat. He coughed, slid open a drawer, came up with a smeared whiskey bottle, half full. He pulled the cork with yellowed teeth, spat it across the room, swigged from the bottle. And all the time the black eyes stayed on Cramer's face.

'You're the law,' Joel Cramer said patiently as Jackson's Bend's marshal slammed the bottle down on the desk and belched. 'It was one of Manson's men damn near cut my wife in half with a scattergun. Wore a mask. Ice-blue eyes, hair like dirty straw. Had a partner been in a knife fight sometime, near lost an eye. Now, that's before we get anywhere near Manson's, Marshal. If there's two men like that on his payroll, you figure that's coincidence — or me tellin' the truth?'

'Where'd this happen?'

'Ten miles out of town. West bank of Jackson's Creek.'

'Manson's land — or a slice of Padraig Flynn's Blue Stack spread if you dig deeper.'

'What I heard, that's all free range.'

Cramer's words were brushed aside as one of the thick hands moved across the desk, came to rest on a thick pile of dog-eared Wanted dodgers.

'Homesteader.' The fat lawman nodded, mouth twisted with contempt, eyes suddenly cruel. 'One of them sod-busters. I heard Manson was having a spot of trouble. Nothing serious. Nothing he couldn't handle . . . '

'I aimed to run cattle,' Cramer said through his teeth. 'I'd been there six weeks, it takes time.'

'Maybe. But I ain't prepared to go harassing a local cattleman on the say-so of a sodbuster name of . . . what was your name agin?'

'Cramer. But that's got — '

'Yeah, Cramer.' The shiny button eyes stayed fixed on Cramer's face while the blackened finger-nails deliberately riffled the papers. 'What I figured when I saw that Colt six-gun with its shiny butt, worn low, tied down real neat. Though that don't bring me any closer to understanding. Joel Cramer, gunslinger. Wanted down on the Rio Bravo for robbery and murder.' His hand moved to the whiskey bottle, pushed it aside. 'They call you Tucson, ain't that right? You want me to sift through these dodgers, Cramer, find a particular one I know's in there, invite you to step out back where we've got

14

strap-steel cells stong enough to hold hard men like you till the circuit judge — '

'That's no way to find the killers,' Cramer cut in, and now his voice was weary. 'For some damn reason you're holdin' a pistol to my head. Maybe you and Manson are in cahoots. But what can either of you gain from murdering a woman, stealing a child?'

'Dyke Manson's a 'breed, moved down from the Nations, and that ain't likely to make us close pards.' The lawman leaned across the desk, jaw jutting as he glared at Cramer. 'But as the elected law in this town I'm bound to protect his interests against your kind. All I've got is your word for what happened. And I still ain't worked out what an Arizona gunslinger's doin' masqueradin' as a sodbuster and hollerin' murder. That alone's justification for holdin' you on suspicion.'

'Suspicion of what?'

'Give me a month with you settin' in that cell, I'll come up with something.'

15

The marshal laughed without mirth. 'Unless, of course, you decide to leave town right now, get the hell out of Jackson's Bend and out of my hair.'

'Maybe I'll do that.'

'Only three choices, ain't none of them pretty. Ride out, or I'll slam you inside so's you can stew waitin' for the hangrope. If I can't manage that without raisin' a sweat, by God I'll shoot you down like a dog, hitch what's left to a hoss and drag your carcass through the dust to Boot Hill.'

3

The marshal's words hung heavy in the silence. Cramer climbed to his feet, his chair scraping. He listened to the old swivel chair groan as the gross, unwashed marshal took his weight off the desk and leaned back, reaching for the bottle, then turned away in disgust and stepped out of the squalid office into the cool, clean air.

He crossed the wide rutted street where the dust of his passing was quickly whirled away by the fickle breeze, knowing as soon as that sweet morning air began clearing his head that he was making a mistake searching for hidden depths in the man. The marshal wanted him out of town in a hurry because it was a damned sight easier than raising a reluctant posse to hunt down a couple of dangerous killers. His job was an easy ride on a lame horse called Jackson's Bend. No doubt he ambled over to the saloon most nights of the week, puffed out his barrel chest with his back up against the bar, a jolt-glass in one hand and his other hooked in his gunbelt, played a few hands of poker with Manson and maybe took a small slice of the cattleman's working profits on the condition that he earned his ordinary wages by doing nothing more energetic than sit in his shabby office drinking rotgut whiskey.

Well, he'd said leave town, and that, Cramer thought wryly, was what he'd always intended. It just so happened that he'd do it in his own good time, and the direction he'd take was not one likely to ease the marshal's troubled frame of mind.

Cramer reached the far plankwalk, stepped up where the smell of frying beef drifted in a hot blue haze from the open door of the town's only eating place — JOE'S GOOD LUCK RES-TAURANT — and took a moment to roll a cigarette and glance about him as the first light of the rising sun began to bathe the street and banish the chill.

Jackson's Bend was a settlement its forgotten founders had raised out of the Kansas prairie between the Smoky Hill and Pawnee rivers some forty miles north of Dodge City. Its one main street was flanked by twisted frame buildings constructed of warped planks held in place by rusting nails and hidden behind lofty false fronts that creaked and swayed in the wind. Of maybe a round dozen seedy commercial buildings, two were saloons serving up liquor that would fell a steer, another was Joe's diner where steak and eggs were the staples. Like the saloonists, Joe was a rarity in a town that had lost his way: they were successful businessmen, because everyone — resident or drifter — has to eat and drink. The other nine premises were not so lucky. They were left to attend to the less pressing needs of maybe a couple of hundred permanent inhabitants who were either too poor or bereft of hope to pack up and move to a better life.

Cramer had ridden by at a distance on his way out to the prairie with Fran and the boy, picked up supplies from Jackson's Bend's general store once in the past six weeks and spent fifteen minutes washing off the smell of the town in Jackson's Creek as soon as he got back home.

But with his family torn apart and his home burned down to the ground out of which its sod walls had been hacked he was now left with no choice. His belly was rumbling, he was in urgent need of a hot bath and a shave and, with a final glance along to the tonsorial, he flicked away the half-smoked cigarette, stepped inside the empty café and placed his order.

'Set a while,' he said a couple of minutes later as the huge, aproned man placed a tin plate of beef and eggs and a steaming cup of coffee before him. He took out his tobacco sack, placed it on the table, and ate his breakfast in silence while the restaurant's bearded owner grunted his thanks then sat across from him, sleeved the sweat from his face and fashioned a cigarette.

'Couple of questions,' Cramer said, his mouth full.

'Fire away.'

'If I wanted to talk to Dyke Manson, which way would I ride?'

'North until you come across a sign nailed to a tree reads Pueblo. Another mile you'll see the ruins of a big barn, a corral with most of its poles lyin' in the dust and a house looks like its owner started buildin' and ran out of cash and energy.'

Cramer paused, frowning, his fork halfway to his mouth. 'I was talking to the marshal. He said something about Manson bein' a cattleman.'

'Yeah, well, he probably also tried hard to convince you he's an officer of the law . . . '

Finch let the words hang, trickled smoke and waited.

'Meanin' he ain't, and Manson's

puttin' on a front?'

'Oh, Butch Farrall's got a right to the badge he's got pinned to his chest. He just don't know what to do with it. Same goes for that 'breed. He's got land, he's got cattle, but he don't know how to put the two together to make 'em pay so that's as close as he'll ever get to bein' a rancher.'

Cramer put down his utensils, pushed away his plate and sat back.

'So if he ain't makin' good use of the land, why's he so keen to get rid of the nesters moved in along Jackson's Creek?'

Finch sucked his teeth, his eyes pensive as he took in Cramer's blood-stiffened shirt.

'That's one helluva lot of questions you're askin'. I know Manson, but . . . Has he done something real bad? Your first call was at the jail. You federal law, or what?'

'Nope. Until around midnight last night I was one of those nesters. Had a wife, a fine son near nine-months old.

Then two of Manson's men came bustin' in, gunned down my wife, took the boy . . . '

Cramer broke off, shook his head, used both hands to lift his cup and stared unseeing into scalding liquid that was like a mirror reflecting the darkness in his tortured soul.

In the strained silence broken only by the sizzle of meat frying out back, a horse clattered past, close up against the plankwalk, the shadow of horse and rider thrown large across the grimy, half-curtained window by a bright morning sun still low on the horizon. In that time, as Cramer regained his composure and looked up, he detected a change in the man across the table, a hooded wariness in the man's eyes.

Those eyes now strayed to the holster resting on Cramer's thigh. Abruptly, Finch lumbered to his feet.

'No sodbuster I ever saw wore a pistol that way. No sodbuster got warned off by Manson's crew ever came a'lookin' for him.' He pushed the

Bull Durham across the table. 'Thanks for the makings. I don't know what you're up to, feller, but I've got work to do.'

'What I'm up to is feelin' my way to the truth,' Cramer said, pocketing his tobacco, 'and so far, from this town, I've got precious little help.'

But Joe Finch had disappeared behind his counter. A tuneless whistle commenced, drowned by the clatter of tin pans. Joel Cramer pushed back his chair and climbed to his feet. Out on the plankwalk again, eyes now squinted against the light, he cast a precautionary glance across the street at the jail then tried to figure out what had caused the sudden change in Joe Finch's manner.

It seemed like every time Manson's name was mentioned, someone was prepared to leap to his defence. According to the marshal, he was a no-account 'breed down from the Nations. Joe Finch was of the same opinion, yet for some reason both of

24

them were prepared to overlook a clear case of murder and kidnapping, by two men who Cramer was convinced worked for Dyke Manson.

A woman had been murdered. A happy kid less than a year old had been spirited away into the night. If the aim had been to drive one more sodbuster off Jackson's Creek, Manson could have wiped out the family and had done with it. But, as Cramer set off along the plankwalk towards the tonsorial parlour, he knew there had to be something more behind this business than ridding the range of a handful of farmers. Maybe doing that was Manson's excuse, but he must have known there was the risk, sooner or later, of a grieving sodbuster taking up his pitchfork, maybe even a battered old Henry repeater, and setting out to hunt down the killers.

Evidently, Manson had decided the prize in the deadly game he was playing was worth that risk. What he couldn't have known was that the day of reckoning had come. Manson, Cramer thought grimly, would pay dear.

* * *

When Joel Cramer finally gravitated towards Ike Goldfink's saloon, it was close to midday and there were now several horses dozing at the hitch rail. As his boots thudded on the plankwalk and he caught a glimpse of his reflection in the saloon's big windows he realized with no surprise that he cut a strange figure: tall and broad-shouldered, six-gun slung low on his thigh, chin freshly shaved, face shining from soap and water and with his dark hair swept back under his Stetson and still damp from the bath — yet still he wore the blood-encrusted shirt, the dark brown stain on its front clearly visible under his open vest.

And a moment later, pushing through the swing doors into the saloon's shadowy interior where cigarette smoke hung in the slanting sunlight and the air was heavy with the odours of stale beer and sweat, he admitted to himself that he had made the unconscious decision to wear that shirt as a personal flag of battle, a clear signal of his intentions to those guilty men who alone would understand its meaning.

Look into men's eyes, he told himself as he stepped up to the bar. Watch reactions. All men with ice-blue eyes or disfiguring knife scars were not killers but, when they encountered him, the guilty ones of that breed would be unable to look at his bloodstained shirt without a flicker of foreboding crossing their countenance, a gloved hand's instinctive drift towards a filled holster.

He ordered whiskey, watched as the bottle was taken down from a rickety shelf and the drink poured by a gangling, swarthy man with a dark, straggling moustache, tossed back the raw liquor and felt it burn his throat but fail to shift the ache that was a terrible sadness. He nodded wordlessly to the aproned saloonist. The glass was refilled and, with it clutched in his hand, he turned around to face the room.

Most of the drinkers had moved along the rough lumber bar to stand close to the massive, pot-bellied iron stove, for the dirt floor was ice-cold and the warmth of the sun had not yet penetrated the shadows. A gambler in a crumpled check jacket was sitting alone at a central table, idly spinning a keno goose. A trio of middle-aged town loafers were seated at another playing solitaire, two smoking and watching while a scrawny oldster turned the cards.

No scars. No ice-blue eyes.

Conscious of the rail-thin man behind him, the squeak of cloth on glass, Cramer said without turning, 'Any of Manson's men in town?'

'Only bit of town I kin see is what you're lookin' at.'

'All right, are there any in here?'

'Frank Cooper with Flynn's Blue Stack riders, a long ways from home

28

— to say more than that, I'd need to know every man's business.'

'You been this close-mouthed all your life, Goldfink?'

'As far as it's gone — and I ain't about to change for no stranger.'

As Cramer brooded over his glass, the gambler spun the keno goose with a final rattling whirr, sprang from his chair and walked over to the bar. He ordered beer, accepted the filled glass, took a slow drink then winked at Cramer.

'Manson's men're too busy movin' nesters off the big 'breed's land to hit town. Ike would've told you, only Farrall's under orders hisself, threatened to close him down. You lookin' for anyone in particular?'

'Keep your mouth shut, Jak,' the saloonist snapped.

'Like I said, he's scared of Butch Farrall,' the gambler said to Cramer. He was a small dark man, dapper but gone to seed, his strong, slender hands restless. Cramer guessed he had a derringer tucked away in the once fancy jacket; hidden danger, of the kind that put a man off-guard with results that could prove fatal. But it was more than a guess. Memories were stirring, and he knew he'd seen this man, long ago, a hazy, pint-sized figure emerging from a pall of gunsmoke, or mist . . .

'Farrall!' There was scorn in the bartender's voice. 'Ain't Butch Farrall bothers me, and you know it!'

'Someone's botherin' every damn one of you,' Cramer said, and watched the little gambler's eyes twinkle with amusement. 'I mention Manson's name, it's like I've developed the plague.' He spun around, caught the bartender glowering at the gambler and said, 'Farrall wants me out of town; gone. If he don't scare you, it's because you're toeing some sort of line. But what's the purpose of that line? Who dug his heel in the dust and scraped that mark? Does that bring us back to Manson?'

'What the hell is it with you and

Dyke Manson?' the bartender said, angrily twisting his cloth inside a glass and glancing towards the doors as they slapped open to admit big Joe Finch. 'You got something against 'breeds?'

'Take a look at his shirt,' the little gambler said, watching Cramer. 'Ask him who died, who did the killin'?'

'Better not.' Finch, the restaurateur, bellied up to the bar and slammed down a coin. 'I just came from the jail. Farrall's busy nailin' a dodger to the notice-board, got a face on him black as thunder, a shotgun in his belt.'

The gambler laughed. 'He'll need more than that for Tucson,' he said, and his dancing blue eyes challenged Cramer.

'It was in Laredo,' Cramer said softly, talking half to himself as he raked the coals of memory. 'Nuevo, west side of the Bravo. Not a derringer. A Winchester. *Rurales* downed my horse. I was pinned against a wall, lamps casting shadows, the warm rain like a heavy curtain . . . ' He shook his head,

31

clearing the cobwebs. 'I remember that rain as gunsmoke — '

'That came, fast enough,' the gambler said, his eyes alight. 'It was the wall of the cantina you were up against. I came out the door to a whore's laughter and the tinkling of guitars, walked into a hail of lead. Two of us then, back to back, a Winchester apiece, that rain hissing on the hot barrels, steam like river mist, then the gunsmoke and we used that and the rain to slip away from that adobe border town . . . '

'Never saw you again,' Cramer said, and extended his hand, grinning.

'Must be, what, fifteen years?' The gambler shook his head in disbelief. 'Jak La Roche,' he said, taking the proffered hand. 'You're Tucson Joel Cramer, and now you're chasing Dyke Manson — God help him!'

4

'You saved my life,' Cramer said, raising his glass to La Roche and receiving a dip of the head in return. 'Once in fifteen years ain't making a habit of it, but if Butch Farrall comes through that door with a shotgun it'll be Nuevo Laredo all over again.'

'This time,' La Roche said, 'I think I'll stand back and watch the action,' and something in his voice made Cramer look hard at the little gambler. But the eyes were still sparkling roguishly, and Cramer nodded slowly, turned to place his empty glass on the bar — and heard the swing doors crash open into a shocked silence.

Across the room the pack of cards spilled to the floor in a greasy, rippling cascade as the man dealing solitaire started with fright. A glass rattled and spun like a fallen coin on the bar, and the moustachioed bartender grabbed for it and swore under his breath.

'I reckon a whole morning's long enough,' Marshal Butch Farrall said, a sawn-off American Arms 12-gauge held high, button eyes glittering and his lardy features set in a grotesque leer as he advanced across the dirt floor to the monotonous, fading slapping of the doors. 'To get out of town all a man needs do is set astride his horse and point its nose in the right direction — but it seems I've got to show you the way, Tucson.'

'Showing a hog to the trough by leading the way is about your limit, Farrall,' Cramer said, and Jak La Roche's laughter, soft yet clear in the deathly hush, was the fierce draught that fanned the smouldering coals of Farrall's anger.

The shotgun swung around, lined up on Cramer's belt buckle. Muscles bulged in the marshal's bewhiskered jaws. A thread of saliva hung glistening from his chin as his eyes narrowed to slits and his big thumb snicked back the hammers. A fat forefinger hooked around the triggers. As the enraged lawman applied pressure, the knuckle turned white, and there was a sudden flurry of motion at the bar as bearded Joe Finch scrambled out of the line of fire.

Behind the heavy planks, Ike Goldfink said nervously, 'Easy now, fellers, easy . . . '

Alongside Cramer, drink rock steady in his hand, Jak La Roche said lazily, 'A double eagle says Tucson Joel Cramer beats the man with the badge,' and over at the card table one of the kibitzers sniggered, made as if to rise, then choked off the sound and changed his mind as Farrall turned his head just far enough to spit in his direction.

'I'll take that bet,' the marshal said — and the whitened forefinger slackened its hold.

'You see, Tucson?' La Roche said. 'Even a two-legged hog has a sense of fair play.'

'I guess it was the thought of that gold coin turned his head,' Cramer said.

'All it means,' Butch Farrall said flatly, 'is I get paid extra for doin' something that'll give me pleasure.' To La Roche, he said, 'You in or out, gamblin' man?'

'I ain't needed,' La Roche said, 'seein' as you'll never get to pull those triggers. Reckon I'll stay right here alongside Tucson, watch you die.'

Farrall's breath hissed through his teeth at the taunt. The button eyes widened, glittering, and out of the corner of his mouth he said, 'You, feller, step over here with them pasteboards.'

Wood scraped across the floor as the scrawny solitaire player, down on his knees gathering the spilled cards, barged into the table in his haste to climb to his feet and obey the lawman. He stepped over, offered the pack to Farrall with a shaking, bony hand, saw a single card slide out of his grasp and made a frantic grab as it

36

fluttered to the floor.

'Leave it!'

There was a savage grin on Farrall's face as the oldster froze, a bony statue uncertain whether to straighten or stay stooped.

'That one don't count, so leave it lie. The next one will. You understand what I'm sayin', gunslinger?'

'The next card our friend lets fall is the signal.' Cramer met the marshal's malevolent gaze and said, 'Do we move when it falls, or when it lands?'

'I'll be charitable,' Farrall said, leering, 'give you another half second of worthless life. When that card hits dirt, you make your draw and I cut you in half with this scattergun.'

Cramer nodded, his eyes suddenly amused. 'Friend,' he said to the trembling oldster, 'I want you to flip through that pack till you come to the ace of spades. When you've got it, step back out of the line of fire, put the rest of the pack on the table and wait for the marshal's word.'

'Hell, I've allowed you extra time so quit wastin' — '

'Humour me.' Cramer's voice was mild as he watched the sweating old man riffle through the pack, locate and draw out the ace of spades and move unsteadily back close to the table. One of the seated kibitzers took the pack from him. The solitaire player held the ace up high, his skinny arm like a reed bending before a strong breeze.

'I guess that's us all set,' Cramer said, and he took a step away from the bar and deliberately looked into the marshal's eyes.

'He never did get the hang of bein' a lawman,' Jak La Roche said sadly, 'and now it's too late.'

'Keep your eye on Goldfink,' Cramer said. 'Most saloonists I've met keep a hideaway weapon.'

And suddenly the tension in the room was like the eerie, sulphurous silence before an electrical storm.

'Last chance,' Farrall said, and now his voice cracked and drifted off key.

'Mine — or yours?'

'I'm givin' you one you didn't have.'

'More charity?' Cramer said, and shook his head in mock disbelief. He stood balanced on the balls of his feet. His body was totally relaxed, his right hand a little way out to the side and hanging loose.

'Your kind,' Butch Farrall said hoarsely, 'just never learn.'

Cramer chuckled. 'A man learns from his betters — and I ain't met one.'

'Damn you, Tucson!' The marshal's voice was tight with strain, his forehead glistening under the greasy Stetson, his big knuckles bone-white on the shotgun. His eyes shifted. He shot a questioning glance at the old-timer, caught the nervous bob of his head.

'All right,' Farrall said, and leaned forward over the shotgun like a man preparing to lunge. 'Let her go, feller!'

The ace of spades slipped from the oldster's knobbly fingers.

Like a dry, dead leaf, it floated down,

39

flipping in the air, exposing first one face then the other.

Its fall was deceptively fast, Tucson Joel Cramer much faster.

The falling card was halfway between the solitaire player's nerveless fingers and the dirt floor when his right hand blurred and came up holding his six-gun. His first shot smashed into the American Arms shotgun close to the trigger-guard and wrenched it from Farrall's grasp. The shattered weapon was still in the air, barrel glinting as it spun to the floor, when Cramer's left hand whipped across his body and fanned the six-gun's hammer. That second bullet plucked the playing card out of the air and sent it whirring across the room like a pale, frightened bird.

Gunsmoke drifted in the shafts of sunlight. Joe Finch coughed drily, like a man having difficulty breathing. In the silence it was possible to hear the steady patter of the blood dripping from Butch Farrell's lacerated fingers, the lazy sounds drifting in through the swing doors from a town that was never fully awake.

Then the man who had slipped away from the table to chase the playing card held up his catch and said softly, disbelievingly, 'It was fallin', spinnin', an' he plugged it plumb centre, drilled a hole clean through the middle of the black spade!'

'That don't make him anything better than a coward for what he done,' Butch Farrall said through clenched teeth.

'Nevertheless,' Jak La Roche said, 'for what he done you owe me twenty dollars.'

A fierce grin split the marshal's glistening face. Blood spattered the card table as he shook life back into his bleeding right hand. He kicked the ruined shotgun across the room and said joyfully, 'It ain't over yet, gamblin' man.'

'I always intended leaving town,' Cramer said, frowning. 'Seems to me you're expending a lot of effort for no reason.'

'A man rode in, stopped at the jail,' Joe Finch called from the end of the bar. 'Spoke to Farrall when he was pinnin' up that sign.'

'You tired of livin', Finch?' Farrall snarled.

'That bit of paper was justification,' La Roche opined. 'The marshal was servin' notice that the man he was about to kill deserves to die.'

'Why the change?' Cramer said, eyeing Farrall with some perplexity. 'First I'm told to leave town; now somebody wants me dead.' He looked down at the pistol, forgotten in his hand, pouched it, and shook his head as he glanced sideways at La Roche. 'You reckon the rider was from Dyke Manson?'

The gambler nodded. 'If that man's running the game,' he said, 'he's upped the stakes,' and Cramer was still holding the little man's mocking gaze and pondering on his words when the roof fell in.

He went down to the sound of a distant singing and the flashing of a white light of such brilliance that he screwed up his eyes in agony. Then his cheek was hard against the cold floor, the taste of earth in his mouth. A hollow roar of rage came to him from an enormous distance and, as his head cleared and the sound of celestial choirs faded, he knew that it was not the saloon's roof that had felled him but the bloody, bludgeoning right fist of Butch Farrall.

Boots scraped, alerting Cramer. He rolled, spitting, tasting Farrall's blood and his own, came up against a pair of legs and the bar's timbers and peered before him, blinking. Farrall had backed off and was gazing in agony at his damaged right hand. The legs belonged to Jak La Roche. Recalling how the gambler had given him no warning, and with a muttered, 'Thanks, feller!' Cramer reached high to grab a handful of the gambler's pants and used them to climb to his feet.

He was halfway up when the enraged Farrall launched himself headlong across the floor. His shoulder slammed like a battering ram into Cramer's chest. The full weight of the marshal's stocky body forced him back, pinning him against the massive bar. Breath whistled from his lungs. Trapped like a beetle against the rough boards, he felt a rib crack. Farrall leaned into him, muscular legs spread and braced, and began to throw short, swinging punches. A bunched fist came over in a high, looping blow that cracked against Cramer's ear and knocked his head sideways. Another vicious body punch drove deep into his belly. Hot shafts of agony knifed into his groin and turned his legs to water.

Cramer sagged heavily across the marshal. Limp, wrung-out, he made use of his own weakness in a desperate attempt to smother the lawman's rhythmic, piston-like punching. Farrall shook himself like a wet dog. At some stage he had lost his hat. Now his head snapped up, cracking against the underside of Cramer's jaw then boring into his exposed throat.

Cramer choked, spat blood. His right forearm was bearing down on Farrall's hulking shoulders. He slid his left arm down between the lawman's chin and chest, brought his hand up, hooked it into the elbow of his braced right arm and began to squeeze.

Butch Farrall growled. Cramer tightened the pressure. The growl became a hoarse rattle, a frantic fight for breath. The lawman eased back, tried to straighten. Then, choking, he began to jerk his torso from side to side, shaking Cramer the way a terrier shakes a rat.

Cramer let his legs go slack and leaned on him, tightened his left arm, kept his right as straight and hard as an iron bar — and squeezed.

Now Farrall began to panic. His boots were firmly planted on the dirt floor. His trunk-like legs were braced, but in them there was a faint tremor.

He went still, somehow held that position for several long seconds while, inexorably, Cramer's stranglehold drained away his strength. Then, with one mighty effort, he strained upwards, lifted Cramer clear of the floor and swung him away from the bar.

Cramer hung on. His weight was too much for the weakened lawman. Farrall tried to shake him off by spinning, lurched sideways, staggered half a dozen paces across the room then went down as his legs crumpled beneath the crushing load. Both men crashed into the card table, scattering the deck of cards and sending the three old-timers leaping backwards. A table leg snapped with a crack like a pistol shot.

But now it *was* all over. Face down, Farrall's nose was mashed against the dirt floor, Cramer's weight across his head and shoulders, his arm clamped across the lawman's windpipe. The seconds ticked away while motes drifted lazily in the slanting sunlight. There was a final, rasping wheeze, a twitch of the heavy legs. Then the marshal's gross body went limp and he lay still.

His head came up then smacked the floor as Cramer carelessly withdrew his arm. He stood up stiffly, became conscious of the blood dripping onto his already stained shirt and dragged his sleeve across his mouth as he looked around the room that seemed still to be catching its breath.

One of the kibitzers was lifting the table and propping it on the broken leg so his friend could get back to his solitary game. The other was holding the ace of spades with the bullet hole punched cleanly through its centre and, as Cramer watched, he tucked it away in his shirt pocket and glared defiance at the card player. But that worthy was in any case in no mood to recommence flipping the cards. With a black look at the unconscious marshal he tugged a battered Stetson down over his grey hair, turned tail and stomped unsteadily out of the saloon.

'And that,' Joe Finch said from the

end of the bar, 'is what I recommend you do, feller.'

'Always been what I intended,' Cramer said. 'I told the man, but he wouldn't listen.' He stepped over Farrall's prostrate form, felt reaction wash over him in a sudden weakness that was like a chill and leaned heavily on the bar.

'Nevertheless,' Jak La Roche said, 'like Nuevo Laredo, this is a town we should leave in a hurry.'

Cramer gestured to Ike Goldfink, then shot a swift glance at the nattily dressed gambler and cocked an eyebrow. 'We?'

'Dyke Manson, remember? You intend tacklin' him on your own?'

Cramer accepted the glass of beer from the sullen saloonist, tilted his head to swallow a long, cooling draught, then gently massaged his bruised jaw and let his tired eyes become unfocused while he pondered on La Roche's words.

By all accounts, Manson was a tough customer, and if Fran's killers were on his payroll then the 'breed employed an equally hard-bitten crew. But Cramer reluctantly admitted that he hadn't given much thought to his next moves. Ride out to the Manson spread, ask questions. That was about as far as his somewhat scrambled thought processes had taken him, and he realized now that La Roche had a point.

'I guess a man who sees his wife cut down before his eyes and his boy taken by the killers has trouble gettin' his thoughts straight,' he said quietly. 'If you've got nothing better to do, I'd appreciate the company of a man I can trust.'

'One incident, fifteen years in the past — and he trusts me!' Jak La Roche spread his hands in mock despair as he looked around the watchers in the saloon, his blue eyes dancing with impish humour. Then, like a light going out, the smile was wiped away. 'So, we'd better make it fast, my friend. I'd hate to be around when our lawman comes round.'

As, indeed, he was. Cramer saw the bulky figure sprawled on the floor twitch, caught the soft whisper of exhaled breath, the choking gasp as the downed marshal sucked in air and began testing his limbs.

'The man needs help,' Ike Goldfink said, and came around the bar with a bucket of water.

'Drown the bastard,' Joe Finch said, and leaned back with his elbows hitched onto the bar to watch.

But as Cramer downed his drink, turned from the bar and led the way past Ike Goldfink to the swing doors, what he didn't see was the way the good humour was wiped from the little gambler's face and his eyes — fixed on Cramer's retreating back — changed from the soft warmth of summer skies to chips of cold blue ice.

5

They left town in a cloud of dust, the angry crackling of a six-gun signalling their departure, the whine of the slugs the spur that drove them to a flat-out gallop that left Marshal Butch Farrall fuming impotently on the edge of the town of Jackson's Bend and, after a long, uphill mile, both the fleeing men's horses badly winded.

'Far enough!' Cramer yelled and, as the trail north topped a rise on which a thin stand of trees offered some shelter from the heat, he waved his Stetson high overhead to signal to the little gambler — a hundred yards ahead and riding like the wind — to pull in.

'No sense breaking our necks hurrying when neither one of us knows where the hell we're headed,' he said as he swung down from the blowing horse, slapped it on the rump and watched it walk away towards the nearest patch of lush Kansas grass.

La Roche was already relaxing in the shade, rolling a smoke. The check jacket had been removed, exposing a blue striped shirt under bright red galluses. From his pants the butt of a six-gun jutted, and it crossed Cramer's mind that a man who carried his pistol in such a manner must be supremely confident, or a fool.

'So, what happened to turn a gunslinger into a sodbuster with a grievance?' the gambler asked as Cramer hunkered down with his back to a tree, trailed tobacco along a paper, rolled and crimped the cigarette and applied flame.

'I met a woman,' Cramer said, watching memories in the trickling smoke. 'We got hitched, and after a while she gave me a fine boy. Then last night I lost both of them in maybe thirty seconds of violence.'

'That explains why you've got a bee in your bonnet over Dyke Manson,' La

Roche said. 'You bein' a nester, and him set on clearing them off his range. But what it don't explain is, why go after him now, and not last night.'

'My wife took a while dying,' Cramer said, remembering how he had cradled her in his arms while her ragged breathing slowed painfully, the tight clutch of her hand as her clear blue eyes dimmed. And then he stared at the end of his cigarette, wondering why this man had chosen to ride with him. A chance encounter outside a Mexican cantina created no lasting bonds. Like he'd said, saving a man's life once in fifteen years didn't constitute a habit. In Nuevo Laredo, La Roche had stepped out of the smoky barroom into a glittering half-circle of *Rurales'* carbines. Then, he had been fighting for his own life as much as Cramer's, but behind today's actions there had to be another reason.

'That takes care of the only important events in my life since Laredo,' he said quietly. 'How about you, La Roche?'

'Even less,' the little man said. 'Over the years I rode north, going steadily downhill. What you saw in Ike Gold-fink's saloon was the end of my lonely road. Then you came through the door with blood on your shirt and a glint in your eye . . . '

He flicked the cigarette away, looked across grass dappled by sunlight and said softly, 'Another rider left town in a hurry, 'bout the same time we did.'

'You had time enough to see that?'

'I was expectin' it. Cut away north-west. Might be headin' for Pueblo — but, then again, he might not.'

'Finch said a rider spoke to Farrall, before he pinned up that dodger. Could be we'll be expected.'

La Roche shrugged. 'Yeah. I guess you were wrong, Tucson. We both know where we're headed.'

'Dyke Manson's,' Cramer said, know-ing that La Roche had not meant that at all; not knowing, yet, the real meaning behind his words. But that would come. For the present there was the unattended business of the two killers, and he said, 'A place called Pueblo. We ride in, we'll be outgunned. The only way to handle it is ask questions, back off when the signs turn bad.'

'Only problem with that approach,' La Roche said, 'is by openin' your mouth you spread all your cards face up on the table. They see your hand, you think they're gonna let you walk away from there?'

'Thinking is what I ain't done too much of,' Cramer said bluntly. 'Last night I saw a man with cold blue eyes, another with a knife scar, watched what they did to my family and let them ride away. I meet them again self-preservation'll go out the window, my satisfaction'll come from takin' the two of them with me . . . '

'Not with your boy out there somewhere,' La Roche pointed out, and

Cramer climbed to his feet and walked to his horse with his jaw set, knowing the little gambler had — in his own terms — recognized the value of the killers' hole card that made Tucson Joel Cramer vulnerable.

'Then I've got maybe ten miles to come up with a fresh idea,' Cramer said tightly. He swung into the saddle, wheeled out of the trees and rode fast down the far slope of the rise, and was heading north at a fast canter towards Dyke Manson's Pueblo before Jak La Roche was on his feet and slipping into his jacket.

★   ★   ★

After twelve miles they passed the sign Joe Finch told Cramer he would see nailed to a tree, rode through ragged, hock-high grass to where a rough pole corral kept a band of ragged broncs from running free, crossed a trampled dirt yard in the leaning shadow of a ramshackle barn with gaping doors and

56

drew rein in front of a house that was tarpaper and warped timber under a sod roof.

On the wide gallery fronting the shack, an unkempt figure with long black hair sat rocking gently in a chair as they approached, yet somehow managed to keep the barrel of the shotgun level, its aim steady.

'Message got twisted all out of shape,' Dyke Manson said. 'You was told to get the hell off Jackson's Creek, Cramer.'

'Ain't ten miles or thereabouts far enough?'

Manson spat a brown stream of tobacco juice. 'Would be, only you're travellin' in the wrong direction, friend. Off the creek, off my land, out of my goddamn sight — that's what was meant.' The dark, Indian eyes crinkled. 'Instead, you've made your mark as the first sodbuster ever rode in to get hisself shot.'

'He's the first sodbuster ever rode in with a reputation could do you some good,' Jak La Roche said.

Cramer sat easy in the saddle, watching the 'breed in the rocking-chair ruminate on the gambler's remark. He was a massive man, Dyke Manson, muscles run to fat but without, Cramer surmised, any loss of strength. The greasy black hair was snatched back and tied loosely at the neck with a rawhide thong. A black shirt was tucked into black pants white to the knees with dust and tucked into short moccasins. A wicked-looking knife — long blade naked — was thrust through the belt encircling the man's thick waist. That, and the shotgun, were the only weapons in view. It seemed, Cramer thought cynically, the season for shotguns.

Manson pushed against the boards with his foot, set the chair rocking, creaking. His cold eyes lifted to fix on Cramer.

'Came across an hombre, six, maybe seven year ago up in the Nations, little town called Stillwater. Five men rode in, gunned down the town constable.

Two of 'em held the horses, the others walked into the bank to withdraw some cash. They'd have made it clear across the Cimarron with maybe ten thousand dollars, only a feller walked out the saloon across the street and for some damn reason decided it was his business.' The heavy jaws chomped on the tobacco wad. The dark eyes looked Cramer up and down. 'Went by the name of Tucson,' Manson said, 'or so I heard.'

'The odds seemed favourable, and I kinda liked that old Indian wore the badge,' Cramer said, looking at La Roche. 'One man, black hair, built like a log cabin. Another . . . ' His gaze returned speculatively to Manson and he said, 'Yeah, I guess that was you.'

'There was two of us got away, empty handed,' Manson said, 'and now you're here, at the wrong end of a shotgun.'

'He was at the wrong end of Butch Farrall's shotgun a couple of hours ago,' La Roche said, 'and now, here he is.'

The 'breed stirred, spat, squinted across at La Roche. 'So maybe I could use him. But that leaves you out in the cold, tinhorn.'

'Ask him,' La Roche said, his face tightening. 'Him and his reputation would've been dead fifteen years, wasn't for me.'

'It's true,' Cramer acknowledged. 'And if you want nesters cleared off your land, you need men who know what they're doin'.' He turned in the saddle, bridle jingling as he looked across the yard at the derelict barn with its sagging doors wide open to expose the shadowy interior; twisted the other way towards the low-slung bunkhouse set against trees and encroaching undergrowth.

A man had emerged, scratching, undershirt hanging loose outside his pants, to swill his face in a wooden water bucket. Another, similarly dressed, was sitting slouched on a log, his back against the timber walls as he smoked a cigarette and watched the group at the house. Both men looked as if they'd crawled out of bed, but still they wore gunbelts, the holsters tied down.

'If that's the best you can do . . . ' Cramer let the contempt creep into his voice to rile Manson, dismissing the two men from his mind because they were both dark and unscarred and he knew he had not yet found Fran's killers.

'Don't take no fancy gunslinger,' Manson said growled, 'to run off a handful of sodbusters.'

'True for most of them. Dan Packham down on the ox-bow might cause you some trouble.'

Manson grunted. He came up out of the chair with a powerful lunge, left it slapping and creaking as he padded with remarkable limberness to the edge of the gallery. He frowned as his dark gaze swept across to the open barn, drifted over to the two men at the bunkhouse, came back to Cramer. He took a breath, spat, nodded.

'Packham I've heard about.' He jerked a thumb at the bunkhouse. 'Don't be fooled by their looks. Their kind had you running scared, Cramer. In Stillwater you had luck on your side. That won't happen again.'

'So, is that a yes or a no?'

Manson chuckled. 'If it was no, this would've done the talkin',' he said, waggling the shotgun. 'You and your pard stick around. We ride on Packham tonight and I'm a coupla men short. This raid has been planned for some time, so maybe they'll turn up . . . '

The big 'breed shrugged, turned away, tossed the shotgun onto the rocking-chair, picked up a gallon jug standing alongside one of the runners and disappeared into the house.

'Who in hell,' La Roche said as they walked their horses over to the corral and pulled in against the rails, 'is Dan Packham — and why are you so unconcerned about helpin' drive him out of his home?'

'Get this,' Cramer said tersely. 'To

find my boy I'll tread roughshod over anyone gets in my way, make use of every man in this part of Kansas.' He swung down, quickly stripped his rig then turned his mount loose in the corral. As he watched it trot away he said, talking mostly to himself, 'I figured maybe he was here . . . But there's surely no reason for him to be in this godforsaken hole . . . '

'You come up with a reason, you'll find your boy.' La Roche slapped his mount on the rump to send it on its way, stared hard at Cramer. 'So Dan Packham's a means to an end? By helpin' move him on you become part of this wild bunch, privy to secrets?'

'Packham's an owlhoot, lookin' for a place to hole up within reach of Abilene, and the Kansas Pacific railroad. Rode in with a couple of pals, took over a soddy vacated by a family moved on by Manson's persuasive methods. He gets run off, Kansas'll be a whole lot cleaner. So, we do like the man said, and stick around.'

The gambler nodded. 'You figure those two men that's missin' are your killers.'

'A fortnight ago they rode with Manson to warn me off Jackson's Creek. Last night they wore masks, but I recognized them. Now they ain't here. Sooner or later they'll come ridin' in, and when they do, by God! they'll pay dear for their crime — but before that, they'd better come up with some answers.'

'D'you notice,' La Roche said, thoughtfully hefting his rig, 'how our Injun friend neglected to say what'd happen if they do turn up?'

Without answering, Cramer waited until the gambler had hoisted his saddle onto the corral's sagging top pole, then picked up his bedroll and rifle and set off across the yard. Sure, he'd noticed. But something ugly in the 'breed's eyes, the hard edge to his voice, had told Cramer that wherever those two men had gone, whatever it was they had done, it was without

64

Dyke Manson's knowledge.

The big 'breed was as puzzled as Cramer. And as he strode ahead of the little gambler, spurs chinking, no matter which way he looked at it Cramer couldn't reconcile that with what had occurred in town. A man had ridden into Jackson's Bend and spoken to Butch Farrall. The message he carried had sent Farrall after Cramer with a shotgun. The link between the two killers and the 'breed suggested the rider had been sent by Dyke Manson, but if Manson was as much in the dark as Cramer . . .

If . . . And even as he was convincing himself that the 'breed, Dyke Manson, was not involved in the snatch of his boy, he knew deep down that he could be wrong and that, either way, right or wrong, he had not seen the last of the big man from the Nations.

The interior of the bunkhouse was dim and dusty, its crumbling sod roof adding a rank, earthy odour to an atmosphere stinking of tobacco, unwashed clothes and stale sweat. A shaft of sunlight followed Cramer inside, casting his shadow long and revealing a row of bunks down the side of the room where windows were covered by slatted shutters, a central table with tin plates and the remains of a meal, at the far end an iron stove with a chipped coffee pot.

Then the hard brilliance of the sunlight was cut off as La Roche stepped inside and kicked the door shut, and out of the gloom a mocking voice drawled, 'That poor sodbuster Dan Packham'll be shakin' in his boots when he sets eyes on these two mismatched galoots.'

Aware that La Roche had ghosted to one side, Cramer headed for the bunks under the windows and said, 'The sun's only just reached the top of its climb but already I'm kinda tired of tough *hombres* lookin' for sudden death.' His bedroll landed on an empty bunk with a thud. He turned to face the two men sitting at the far end of the table, reached into his shirt pocket for his tobacco sack and sent it skidding along the table towards them. 'Build a smoke. I'll try some of that coffee. If it don't kill me, we can set and talk about absent friends.'

Hooves rattled in the yard, a gruff voice called out, and Cramer reached across the bunk to push open a stiff-hinged shutter. The yard had dried after the overnight rain, and dust was rolling in a yellow cloud. Three men had ridden in, wheeled their horses in front of the house, then dismounted to clatter up the steps and disappear inside.

Cramer pulled at the shutter, decided to leave it open, and turned back to the room.

'Those friends I mentioned,' he said, 'are still absent. Who just rode in?'

'Two of 'em are Manson's kin. The rawboned man with the Mex sombrero's the feller he calls foreman.'

'But you don't?'

The man who had answered slid the

tobacco sack back down the table, blew smoke towards the sagging sod roof, showed a mouthful of yellow teeth in a sardonic grin.

'A foreman gives orders to ranch hands,' he said, 'not hired guns.'

'Ain't that what Manson's aimin' to establish?' Cramer said, sitting down. 'A cow outfit? There's got to be some reason for him grabbin' a chunk of prairie and makin' it his own exclusive territory.'

'Manson heard about all them steers bein' driven up the Chisholm Trail, came down from the Nations to grab hisself a slice. But he ain't gonna spend no hard-earned cash on Texas cows. Him and his kinfolk are hirin' gun-slingers, not cowpokes; the only thing that ramrod's ever bossed is an owlhoot band ran wild around the Texas Panhandle.'

'So what we're lookin' at,' Jak La Roche said with interest, 'is the settin' up of a rustlin' outfit with the cold-blooded aim of stealin' beef on the hoof from worn-out Texas drovers.'

'Leave it,' Cramer said impatiently. 'Manson's get-rich plans don't concern me.' He looked at the second man, dark, silent and watchful, and said, 'Manson told me he's two men short. They got names?'

'Lawson and Wood,' the gunman said, and picked a shred of tobacco off his lip. 'If it's any of your business.'

'It is if one of them's got blue eyes and hair like straw, the other a knife wound ruined one of his eyes.'

'Close enough,' the first man said. He was watching Cramer carefully, and now he said, 'Lawson's the one with the knife scar and the eye mostly white. But you didn't pick them out of the bunch of us rode down to warn you off Jackson's Creek two weeks back, so you must've seen 'em more recent. They were all tensed up and pretty close-mouthed when they rode out last night. I guess a man don't need to think too hard to work out where they went.'

'Keep talking,' Cramer said tightly.

The man shook his head, glanced uneasily at his swarthy companion. 'I've said enough. It was dark when they rode out in the rain, this morning their bunks was empty. You need to know what happened in between, best talk to Lawson and Wood.'

In the ensuing tense silence, Cramer began rolling a smoke while Jak La Roche sat down at the table, pulled a deck of cards from his jacket pocket and dealt a solitaire layout. The snap of the cards as he began to play were insignificant sounds, but in the unusual stillness each card turned was an irritation, the pause between each play serving to heighten the tension.

After a few minutes the dark man swore fiercely, pushed back his chair with a crash and stormed away from the table to an untidy bunk in the corner. There he pulled on a rough cotton shirt, making no attempt to disguise his anger, then made a deliberate show of checking the weapon in the heavy gunbelt buckled about his waist.

'Just so's every man knows where he stands,' La Roche said calmly and without looking up, 'the man askin' the questions is Tucson Joel Cramer, my name's Jak La Roche — and whether you two like it or not, tonight we're ridin' with you to Jackson's Creek.'

A card went down with a crisp snap.

'That's us taken care of,' Cramer said, watching the silently fuming man by the bunk. 'Now, we've got a long day to get through, so why don't we all spend some of that time gettin' acquainted and maybe exchangin' views?'

For a long half-minute the dark gunslinger seemed about to object as he stood with his hand brushing his holster. Then he let go his pent-up breath, wiped his hands on his pants and shrugged.

'I guess I get riled when a stranger walks in, asks too many questions.' He glanced across at the other, silent gunslinger, said, 'I'm Jake Gittins. Feller settin' there's Abe Hawker.'

71

'They friends of yours,' Cramer said, 'this Lawson and Wood?'

'Hell, no!' Gittins wandered back to the table, sat down. 'Not them, nor Dyke Manson.'

Abe Hawker ground out his cigarette. 'So, what have Lawson and Wood done to get your pants in a twist, bring you snoopin' around Pueblo?'

Cramer reached across La Roche's solitaire layout, moved the deuce onto the ace of spades, said quietly, 'Murdered my wife, took my kid — though God knows what for.' He looked from Hawker to Gittins, said, 'I was convinced they were workin' for Manson. Today, in town, it seemed like Butch Farrall was followin' instructions, and again I couldn't see beyond Dyke Manson.' He let the words soak in, saw no reaction and went on, 'I was disinclined to believe the big 'breed when he denied all knowledge. But since you both confirmed what he said, I'm forced to change my line of thinking.'

'Lawson and Wood were hired by Manson,' Hawker said. 'Rode in maybe a month ago, like they was saddle-tramps ridin' the chuck-line.' He stood up, lifted the coffee pot off the stove, offered it to Cramer who extended a grubby tin cup and watched the stream of black coffee. 'But a man only needs to look at the way they wear their six-guns to know their trade, and in the time they've been around they've kept themselves to themselves.'

'Other absences, before last night?' Cramer asked over the cup of lukewarm java.

'Once or twice. Never this long.'

'And no ideas about where they went?'

'Left them to it.' Hawker splashed coffee into a cup, tasted it, pulled a sour face. 'They were around when there was action — you're witness to that. What they did other times was their business.'

'What about *dinero*?' La Roche

73

asked, raking in the cards and shuffling the deck.

'Not short,' Jake Gittins said, frowning. 'Manson pays on time, but I'd say the both of 'em had more than he was handin' out.'

'That's pure guesswork,' Hawker objected.

'Nah.' Gittins shook his head. 'Coupla times you were in town, Manson's kin came across from the house, the five of us played poker. Lawson and Wood lost both times, settled up with gold coin Lawson carried in a leather pouch.'

'Possible they brought it with them,' La Roche suggested.

Again Gittins was adamant. 'The day Manson signed them up, I overheard them talkin'. Lawson was on about the cartwheel he keeps hid in his boot. That's what they were down to, one silver dollar.'

Harsh voices rang out, and through the open shutters Cramer watched the two men he'd been told were Manson's kin mount up, swing their horses away from the house and ride out. The tall man wearing the black sombrero, Manson's *segundo*, roared out from the gallery steps, 'Gittins, Hawker, get out here and see to the horses!'

Two minutes later, after a brief flurry as the two men pulled on their duds, Cramer and La Roche were alone in the bunkhouse.

'No wiser than when you left town,' La Roche said.

'Some.' Cramer got to his feet to pace restlessly, lifted the coffee pot, put it down with a clatter, turned to walk back down the room. 'I know the boy ain't here; I know Lawson and Wood are involved in something outside of Pueblo.'

'You call him the boy,' La Roche said quietly, the deck of cards squared in his fine-boned hand forgotten as he turned his head to watch Cramer. 'Not once have you mentioned his name.'

'Nor will I,' Cramer said tightly, 'until he's back where he belongs.'

'That, and the bloodstained shirt stays on your back,' La Roche said, nodding, and for a few minutes the only sound was the light tread of Cramer's boots on the dirt floor, the riffle of cards as the little gambler idly practised one-handed cuts and two-handed passes.

Finally, Cramer took a deep breath, sat down across from La Roche, began rolling a cigarette.

Staring down at the deck of cards, La Roche said, 'Something stuck in my mind, all those years. I walked out of that bar into a circle of guns and took your side, but I never did find out why the *Rurales* had you pinned down.'

A match flared. Cramer inhaled, trickled smoke, eyes inward. 'In those days,' he said, 'I was an explosive bundle of mostly hot blood and muscle ridin' a wiry bronc, an immature kid who thought a fast six-gun made him God. Every one of them damn *Rurales* was a killer or bandit fresh out of a Mexican jail.' He looked through the hanging smoke at Jak La Roche. 'Nuevo Laredo had more than one *cantina* where Mex peasants strummed guitars and bottom-card mechanics fleeced drunken strangers. I guess the feller plyin' his dishonest trade where I was drinkin' didn't look into my eyes.'

'You killed him,' La Roche said.

'Stone dead,' Cramer said. 'It was only then I found out he wasn't packing a pistol,' and he saw Jak La Roche's hands tighten on the deck of cards, and wondered why.

6

It was raining again when they rode out, a thin night drizzle that held the warmth of a summer day in its moisture and left every man damp and sweating before the war-party had covered a mile. Theaker, the ramrod, rode point with his black sombrero ducked against the rain, but of Manson and his kin there was no sign and Cramer guessed that when he was all done with warnings the big 'breed left the mopping up to his hired guns.

Before leaving Pueblo they had briefly exchanged words, Theaker, Cramer and La Roche, but if the ramrod was impressed by reputations — Tucson's or Dan Packham's — he had no difficulty keeping his feelings hidden.

'We reach the creek,' he'd said

gruffly, 'just listen to what I say, follow my lead.'

'You know this Packham?' Cramer had asked, and the gaunt man's eyes had glittered evilly in the deep shadow under his wide-brimmed hat giving both Cramer and La Roche the feeling that this rangy gunslinger followed his chosen profession for love, not money.

They covered the ten miles of mostly open prairie in an hour, under thinly overcast skies lit from above by the high, floating moon. Each man rode with the group, but apart. Each man was alone with his thoughts. In the final mile the tension mounted. From the crest of the final, grassy slope the waters of Jackson's Creek shone like a ribbon of steel beyond a line of cottonwoods that extended north and south along the west bank. The soddy occupied by Dan Packham was a shapeless mass abutting a dark hillock of raw earth covered by patches of wet grass.

As the big ramrod raised his right hand the riders came together in a steaming group of blowing horses and jingling bridles, Gittins alongside Hawker, La Roche a little apart from Cramer who had moved up to Theaker's stirrup.

'Four horses tied up at that hitch rail he's got rigged,' the ramrod said, and there was an element of surprise in his voice as he looked at Cramer. 'You and him got warned the same night. At that time there was just Packham and a worn out Texan wrangler.'

'I asked if you knew him,' Cramer said, 'and you played dumb. So now I'm tellin' you. Packham's an outlaw, chose Jackson's Creek because it's close to Abilene and the railroad. Christ knows what he's got planned, but it stands to sense he's gonna need more than one tired horse-breaker.'

A cool wind had picked up, stirring the wet grass, lifting the horses' manes. Saddle-leather creaked as Theaker eased his weight, lifted a hand to settle his big sombrero. He was looking down the slope to where yellow lamplight glowed in the square hole that was the soddy's window, and Cramer sensed the uneasiness in the big man. Manson's *segundo* was accustomed to raids such as this being an easy ride against stubborn men and their terrified families: a sodbuster tired from a long day's work, undernourished children clinging to their mother's skirts. But now there was uncertainty, a foreboding created by the sight of four tethered horses . . .

Then a rifle cracked, cutting through Cramer's thoughts. Gittins swore softly and went down with his horse as it sank to the ground, and in that moment Joel Cramer knew he had found the two men, Lawson and Wood.

'You were right,' he said to Theaker. 'They did turn up, only on the wrong side.'

But a fierce volley of shots buried his words in the crackle of gunfire. Slugs whistled all around them and, as the men ducked down and the four remaining horses milled in confusion,

Cramer judged that there was a single gunman maybe a hundred yards out on each side of the soddy, firing up the slope from the poor cover of the cottonwoods.

'Two of 'em on the flanks, the others waitin' for us in the soddy!' Theaker roared, echoing his thoughts. 'Gittins, Tucson, La Roche, take care of them. Hawker, ride with me.'

A bullet tore the big sombrero from his head to be caught and whirled by the rising wind. Then the foreman had spurred his horse and was racing down the slope towards the soddy, closely followed by Abe Hawker on his light grey gelding. At once, muzzle flashes began winking in the now dark square of the window. Theaker's roar of anger trailed thinly on the night air, and the two riders were forced to send their mounts in a swerving, jinking run across the slippery slope to avoid the rain of slugs.

'We ride together,' Cramer said to La Roche, pointing north. 'Split up when we reach the trees.' To Gittins, huddled down behind his dead horse with his Winchester, he said, 'Use that rifle. Keep the man to the south pinned down.'

He took his horse down the slope at a dead run, flattened along the horse's neck, heading for the northern end of the thin line of cottonwoods. La Roche, lighter, mounted on a faster horse, went past him with the check jacket flying like a cape, snapping shots from his .44. Cramer heard a scream from behind him, and guessed Gittins had taken a slug. Then the line of trees was rushing towards him, the muzzle flashes increasing in brilliance, the sinister whine of slugs brushing ever closer, and he peeled away from La Roche to tumble from the saddle and hit the ground at a run with drawn six-gun.

He left the horse to trot away, slipped into the woods with the tang of gunsmoke in his nostrils. Pistol cocked and ready, he slipped like a dark shadow from tree to tree. He was vaguely aware of the crackle of gunfire in the distance, the squeal of frightened horses, the faint sound of men calling out. Cramer closed his ears to those sounds. He was no more than thirty yards from the gunman's position. The man's six-gun banged methodically as he plugged away at La Roche. Muzzle flashes glistened on the wet tree trunks. But no slugs winged towards Cramer, and his mouth twisted in a tight grin as he caught a glimpse of La Roche and realized what was happening.

The little gambler had swerved south towards the soddy as he reached the trees and was now riding at a gentle trot, tight up against the dripping grey-green foliage. This brought him dangerously near to the gunman, but up close the trees gave him better cover. And, like an Indian, he had slipped out of the saddle on the far side of his mount. With one leg hooked over the cantle he was firing under the horse's neck, risking his own to draw the gunman's fire.

All this came to Cramer in brief glimpses as he steadily advanced on the hidden gunslinger. Then a broad wedge of trees was between him and La Roche, and as he again turned his attention to the task ahead a single stride took him into a small clearing and the man was there, down on one knee, his back to Cramer as he snapped shots at the reckless gambler.

Cramer stepped into the open space, called out, 'Drop it, feller!'

The man jerked as if stung, spun around. Off balance, he fell back against a tree, banged an elbow hard against it and, as his arm went numb, he almost dropped his six-gun. Even in the wan light Cramer could see the blond hair, the furious, ice-blue eyes, and as he recognized the man called Wood he felt his throat tighten, experienced a surge of uncontrollable rage.

This was the Manson gunslinger who had held the shotgun, pulled the trigger. This was the man who had killed Fran in cold blood because she had reached for a battered old Henry repeater to protect her child.

Without the masking bandanna the blond gunman's face was lean and lantern-jawed. His thin mouth was twisted in a snarl as he staggered sideways and fought to hold his pistol and bring it to bear on this unexpected threat.

As he watched the man fighting, succeeding, saw the six-gun lift, cold common sense washed away Joel Cramer's hot anger.

No, he thought: for the boy's sake I must take him alive.

But there was only a split second left to him, the killer's six-gun now lined up, the black muzzle threatening to spit fire and death.

Cramer's first shot, fired hastily, took the killer in the right shoulder instead of smashing the pistol from his hand. It slammed him back against the tree, but failed to knock him down. The snarl became a sharp intake of breath, a grimace of agony. Cramer snapped a second shot, but now the man was down, hitting the ground hard with a roar of pain. Cramer's slug clipped splinters from the tree, his third smacked into the wet earth as the gunman rolled desperately. Wet blood glistened on Wood's shirtfront. His blue eyes narrowed to slits of pure ice as he came up on his knees. Somehow he had shifted the pistol to his left hand. He fired from the hip. The bullet clipped Cramer's ear. As hot pain knifed through his head he saw the gunman's savage grin, saw him adjust his aim, saw — as if in slow motion — the whitening of the man's trigger finger, and with a terrible sense of failure Cramer shot him between the eyes.

The gunman's head snapped back. He tumbled over backwards, his legs doubled under him, twitched once and lay still.

As he watched the man breathe his last, a portion of the hope driving Cramer also withered and died. He was done, finished. One of the men who could have told him where his boy had been taken was dead, his own careless shooting had killed him, and the fierce rattle of gunfire in the near distance told him that he had little chance of finding Lawson alive.

Then Cramer's jaw muscles bunched. His nostrils flared as he took a deep, shuddering breath, let it go in an explosive exhalation that was a massive release of tension. Hell, one down was one no-good killer out of the way, and while Theaker and Hawker were still blasting away with six-guns it meant someone out there near the soddy was still alive. With Wood counted out that left Packham, the Texan wrangler — and Lawson. One chance in three that the second killer was still standing — and that was good enough.

With a final glance at the dead killer, Cramer pouched his six-gun and turned away to charge through the trees to the open grassland.

As he crashed through the fringe of

undergrowth and into the open the gunfire ceased, and in the sudden silence he saw La Roche on foot leading his horse, a diminutive figure looking even smaller under the wide, luminous skies. The gambler saw Cramer, lifted an arm and waved vaguely to the south.

'Figured maybe you needed a hand,' he called. 'Far as I can tell Theaker stormed the soddy, gunned down both Packham and the Texan.'

Cramer reached him, panting, took a moment to locate his own horse standing with trailing reins a good hundred yards away up the slope, and summoned him with a shrill whistle. Then, as La Roche quickly swung back over leather, Cramer said, 'Wood's dead. That leaves one killer knows where my boy's been taken. If you reckon Packham and the Texan are dead, that must've been Lawson out on the south flank. Sounded like he plugged Gittins soon after we rode down the slope. If Lawson's alive, he ain't likely to hang around after double-crossing Theaker.'

With a thud of hooves, his horse cantered up and nudged his shoulder with its muzzle. Cramer turned, swept up the trailing reins and quickly mounted. La Roche was already making his way across the foot of the slope, heading along the trees to where two motionless horsemen could be seen outside the black bulk of the soddy. Cramer, using his spurs, swiftly drew alongside the gambler.

'Theaker's lookin' the worse for wear,' he said, squinting ahead.

'Enough bullets' been flyin' to give a man lead poisonin' just by breathin' the air,' La Roche said, and his teeth flashed white as he grinned across at Cramer.

Then they had reached the soddy, and it was plain to Cramer from the *segundo*'s slumped attitude in the saddle that Theaker had taken a slug.

'Bad hurt,' Hawker said, catching his glance. 'Slug in the belly. He shrugged eloquently.

'Get him back to Pueblo, put him on Manson's buckboard,' Cramer said. 'You'll find your pard up the hill. I don't expect he's too healthy.' Then, 'What about Packham and his crew?'

'Him and the Texan wrangler are both dead.'

'And Lawson?'

Hawker moved restlessly in the grey's saddle as the tall foreman swayed, both hands clasped tight on the horn as he cursed softly through his teeth.

'If that was him to the south, he's still around.' He met Cramer's cold gaze, said, 'I guess, seein' as it was you went after him, Wood cashed in his chips?'

La Roche's dry chuckle was answer enough. Hawker nodded acceptance, without emotion. He kneed his horse over to Theaker, leaned across to take the *segundo*'s reins, pulled the horse around to the west.

'You rode into Pueblo askin' enough questions to show where your interests lie,' he said to Cramer. 'For what it's worth, I'm pretty damn sure Lawson

91

took one of my slugs.'

'I should thank you,' Cramer said, and again the mood of helplessness threatened to overwhelm him as he added, 'But if Lawson's dead, my interest died with him.'

7

They watched the gunslinger lead the wounded foreman up the long slope, leaning over every now and then to keep Theaker upright. La Roche spat disgustedly into the grass, said, 'How d'you want this played?'

Cramer grunted. 'Bein' clever won't help. Hawker reckons Lawson's still around. I ain't heard no movement, but what does that prove? If he's got an ounce of sense he would have taken his horse, 'stead of leavin' it tied. Without it he'd be forced to walk away — or it could be he's still in the cottonwoods, waitin' around for Wood.' He shook his head impatiently. 'Too many possibilities, any one of which could be wrong — and while I'm talkin, he could be dyin'.'

'On foot, maybe wounded . . . ' La Roche flicked the reins decisively,

93

moved off towards the cotton-woods. With a thoughtful look at the little gambler's back, Cramer kneed his horse around and followed.

They rode past close to the soddy, their horses' hooves first sinking into the soft earth then scraping on the packed ground close to the hitch rail were the four horses, still tethered, moved nervously at their passing. The acrid smell of gunpowder clung to the shabby dwelling. A short, runty figure was lying sprawled in the open door-way. Dark blood soaked the earth around his head. A six-gun gleamed, a foot away from the clawed fingers of his dead, reaching hand.

'Packham'll be inside,' Cramer said, feeling a sickness in his stomach as he turned his head away from the dead wrangler. 'One good thing to come out of this mess: I had no part in these killings.'

La Roche glanced over his shoulder, eased his horse back so that Cramer could draw alongside. 'I see you've got a well-honed philosophy. You're at the scene, holdin' a pistol, but you didn't fire the fatal shot so there's no blood on your hands?'

'Life's tough enough without gettin' weighed down by unnecessary guilt,' Cramer said, talking for the sake of it while wondering what was coming next.

'Does that apply to the times when it is your finger on the trigger? Like, for instance, that card mechanic you told me you killed down in Laredo?'

'Fifteen years ago,' Cramer said softly. 'The town was full of desperadoes, more people died of knife or bullet wounds than died in bed — so why would one more trouble you?'

'Curious, is all. After what you just said about guilt. He cheated at cards, and that's a form of robbery. So does that — in your eyes — justify what you did? Killing him . . . this card sharp — what was his name . . . or didn't you say?'

They were cutting in close to the trees.

Cramer lifted a warning hand, leaving the gambler's question unanswered as he cocked his head the better to listen in the heavy silence broken only by the uneasy soughing of the wind.

It came again, in among the trees, the faintest of snaps. It was followed by the whisper of metal on oiled leather as Cramer drew his six-gun. They had ridden barely a hundred yards, but he knew there was no use for a horse in timber and, again, he slid from the saddle. The grass was longer here, swishing against his boots and soaking his trousers to the knee.

At his shoulder, also on foot, La Roche said in a low voice, 'I make him no more than thirty yards away, havin' a tough time of it. But in the cotton-woods his eyes'll be sharp, he's heard us and sure as hell he'll pick us out against the light . . . '

'Blind in one eye. And the trees're thinning, pushing him closer to the creek,' Cramer said tightly. 'Walk away,

La Roche, see to the horses, leave this to me. I don't want you blazing away at shadows.'

He slipped silently into the trees, wondering at the instinct that had warned him not to have the gambler at his back, smiling grimly as he heard the fading rustle of grass behind him followed by the jingle of a bridle. Then he dismissed Jak La Roche from his mind and began to inch forwards, with each step testing the ground underfoot before risking his weight, right arm bent, cocked six-gun held high.

The cottonwoods now thinned rapidly. Jackson's Creek was clearly visible to Cramer's left. The light, filtering through the trees, reached ground covered by wet dead leaves so that it shone like the smooth scalp of a balding man. Then his reaching left hand touched a tree trunk that had a different, warmer kind of wetness, a wetness that chilled the soul, not the skin, and when Cramer lifted that sticky hand close to his eyes he saw the darkness of blood.

So, Lawson had taken the slug high up. And losing that much blood, surely a fatal wound.

And then, as he wiped his palm clean on rough bark, he caught the first movement, saw the shadowy figure break clear of the trees and hobble awkwardly along the creek bank.

Not walking right. Shot more than once. High up in the chest, and a bad leg wound.

'Lawson!' Cramer called. 'Hold it right there. You're in no shape to run. Stand still, or I'll cut you down.'

At his cry the wounded killer seemed to leap with shock, half turning so that his legs became tangled and he stumbled sideways towards the flat silver surface of the deep river. His blind eye gleamed milk-white. A pistol glinted in his fist. The flash of the shot was blinding. The bullet hummed close to Cramer's head, snicking through the branches.

Cramer clenched his teeth, lifted his

six-gun as he ran along the edge of the trees with the cold damp smell of river weeds in his nostrils. Lawson seemed disorientated, confused, clearly suffering from pain and loss of blood. He snapped a wild second shot at Cramer's old position, spun dizzily. His third shot winged harmlessly towards the thin, high cloud cover. That third shot almost knocked him flat. The big six-gun jerked, the recoil driving the killer backwards. Cramer saw his legs wobble. Then he was lurching sideways, slipping and sliding down the steeply sloping bank. His arms windmilled as he fought for balance. The six-gun flew from his hand in a glittering arc. His right leg buckled. One final, desperate lunge took him crunching backwards across fine shale. Then he hit the water on his back and went under.

'Goddamn!'

The oath was torn from Cramer's lips as he watched the killer sink below the surface, saw the last slim chance of finding his son drift away with the widening, fading ripples on the slow-moving waters of Jackson's Creek as Lawson drowned.

Swiftly he pouched his pistol, stripped off his gunbelt and boots and charged across the grass. He slithered down the bank and onto the gravel. As he did so, the clouds slid away from the moon and he could clearly see the sluggish waters of the creek. Beneath them, there was no sign of life. Instead, a weak stream of bubbles broke the smooth surface, and on that surface there was an ugly, spreading red stain.

Stepping high, Cramer ploughed into the icy water. The bank shelved steeply. He went in up to his thighs, his groin, caught his breath as the cold knifed through his innards when it reached his waist, stumbled and almost went down as both feet came up hard against the immovable bulk of Lawson's sub-merged body. He turned his face to the side and thrust his arms deep under the surface, found nothing he could grasp; sucked in a deep breath through his open mouth, then held it as he plunged head and shoulders under the cold waters. Blind, groping, his fumbling hands found Lawson's chest. He grabbed handfuls of shirt, braced his thighs, reared up out of the creek with his awful burden.

In the brightening moonlight, Lawson was a ghastly sight. The killer's good eye was sightless, wide and staring, the round, glistening orb of a dead fish. Water poured in glistening streams from his eye sockets, his open mouth. Cramer's clutching hands were stained bright red, blood-stained water a red deluge streaming from the stricken man's clothes.

It took all Cramer's strength to drag Lawson's dead weight a few yards, splashing through deep water to the bank. He dumped him on his back in the wet shale, with hands on thighs and chest heaving he stood gasping and shuddering. Then he dropped heavily to his knees. A single heave sent the stricken man flopping over onto his face. Only for an instant did Cramer hesitate as he thought of the man's terrible wounds, and the damage he was about to inflict. Then he knelt astride the man, planted both hands in the centre of Lawson's back and through straight, braced arms used his whole weight to begin pumping the river water out of the unconscious man.

For thirty long, agonizing seconds, while he kept up the rhythmic pumping, he thought it was too late: Lawson was dead, his own tow-headed son was forever lost.

Then, in a gruesome spasm, the killer heaved, coughed, choked up a stream of water. But this now came from his punctured lungs, not his stomach, and Cramer narrowed his eyes as he saw that the liquid gushing from the gaping mouth and soaking into the wet shale was almost pure blood.

Bracing himself, knowing that time was fast running out, he flipped Lawson over onto his back. And now, as the moonlight struck the killer's wet, bone-white countenance, there was a glimmer of life in that single undamaged eye — not much, nothing to give hope of a future for the man, but at least there was awareness and recognition under the mask of pain — and that gave Cramer hope.

'Where is he?' he panted, his voice ragged and unsteady as he pressed his ear close to the killer's lips. 'Tell me, Lawson, where did you and Wood take my boy?'

And the killer grinned.

Yellow teeth were bared as the lips peeled back. Breath hissed through the red-stained fangs. He tried to say something. His eyes rolled and suddenly, each of them, the blind and the seeing, showed nothing but white and Cramer grasped the dying man's shoulders and shook him, shook him — and the seeing eye steadied, cleared, fixed on Cramer.

'Injuns,' Lawson whispered.

'Indians?' In Cramer's mind, the world rocked, stood still. Unconsciously his hands tightened on Lawson's shoulders, his fingers digging through slack muscle to hard bone, and although life was fast leaking from his body the killer hissed through his teeth at this fresh agony.

'That's where . . . he is . . . '

'What Indians?' Cramer asked — mentally cringing, for in his heart he knew the answer, and was distraught.

'We . . . handed him over . . . to . . . to Quanah Parker's Comanche . . . ' Lawson gasped.

And then his head fell to one side, and he died.

Joel Cramer watched the light fade from the man's eye, heard the rasped exhalation that was followed by nothing but silence and stillness. Moving slowly, painfully, he pushed himself up and, still astride the dead body, settled onto his haunches and let his head fall back until his face was upturned and he was staring blindly up at the night skies.

'And that,' a voice said, 'is the end of

Tucson Joel Cramer's quest.'

When Cramer could bring himself to look, he saw Jak La Roche standing at the edge of the trees. The gambler was holding a pistol, and he meant business.

8

'Riders comin',' La Roche said, and Cramer released his pent-up breath and swallowed hard.

'For a minute, there . . . ' he said huskily, his eyes on the pistol.

'Could've looked bad,' La Roche said, chuckling. 'But think back, Tucson,' he said. 'The way I came out that bar, you encircled by *Rurales* and me blastin' away to save your hide.'

'I'm a mite weary of lookin' back over all that time, and beginnin' to wonder where this is leadin',' Cramer said, climbing off the dead man's body and adding a few more bloodstains to the killer's wet shirt as he bent to wipe his hands. He straightened and cocked his head to listen, measuring the beat of approaching hooves. 'Comin' from Pueblo, not town. Yet Theaker's not fit, and I can't see Dyke

Manson stirring himself.'

'Butch Farrall was bad riled. If he was following you, he'd have gone first to Pueblo. Manson would expect the five of us to have finished Packham by now. He'd have no reason not to point the marshal this way.'

'This'll mean more shooting.' Cramer couldn't keep the weariness out of his voice, but La Roche shook his head.

'Farrall will head for the soddy. He'll find two men dead, no sign of life. This time of night he won't go lookin' for tracks.'

'The horses . . . '

'In the woods, out of sight. We can walk them south, the one direction Farrall won't expect us to take.'

'All right.' Cramer set off for the trees, brushing past close to the gambler and, in doing so, putting out a rough hand to push the man's six-gun aside. 'We'll walk out that way. But when we're clear I'll cross the creek, wait till daylight to talk to someone about them Indians.'

'Why waste time?' La Roche said. 'If Lawson's dyin' words were about Injuns, that points us north.'

'Not us, me,' Cramer said bluntly as they entered the woods and in the gloom one of the waiting horses whinnied softly. 'The search for my boy ain't over, but there's no call for you to risk that kind of death.'

'You and me,' La Roche insisted, close behind him. 'You think I'd walk out on an old pard?'

They were threading their way through the trees. There was a question niggling at the back of Cramer's mind, but it escaped him as he realized that he had again placed himself so that the gambler was at his back.

As if reading his thoughts, La Roche went on, 'A man needs somebody to watch his back, and I ain't got nothing better to do, not now, not later.'

Then they had reached the horses. Each man gathered up the reins and moved away through the cottonwoods. Behind them, at a distance, they heard the hoofbeats slow, the faint whisper of men's voices that even as they listened were raised in anger.

They led their mounts steadily away from those sounds for thirty minutes. During that time they were concealed from view in the strip of cotton-woods that followed the line of Jackson's Creek, first thinning, then widening to become a broad tongue of woodland before abruptly coming to an end where the creek flowed across flatter land and the two men emerged into bright moonlight.

It was long past midnight. The air was chill, the wet ground covered by the skirts of a thin mist that hung low over the creek. The only sounds were of water on shingle, the restless movements of the horses. Cramer's spurs chinked musically as he swung up into the saddle, turned its head towards the water.

'You said Lawson's words pointed to the north,' he said, remembering the question that had eluded him. 'He never mentioned it, so why?'

'There was talk in Goldfink's saloon, between Farrall and a couple of drifters. They'd heard of a renegade group splitting from Quanah Parker's main band of Comanches down in the Panhandle. Happened maybe a year ago. They'd been driftin', crossed to the east side of Jackson's Creek and moved on, but since then they've been in the one place. Braves, squaws, kids.'

'Yeah, that story reached me. But where's this one place they're at?'

'North of Jackson's Bend somewheres.' La Roche shrugged.

'But not all that far. Lawson and Wood took my boy last night, round about supper-time.'

'So, a day there and back, at the outside,' La Roche calculated. 'Maybe less; no tellin' how long they'd been at Packham's soddy.'

'Well,' Cramer said, 'ain't no sense visitin' redskins, wherever they are, when we're plumb wore out. We cross the river, find the nearest stretch of timber and bed down for the night.'

They moved off, mist swirling around the horses' legs as they whispered through the thick wet grass towards Jackson's Creek, and they had negotiated the steep bank, crossed the gravel and were splashing into the water when La Roche said, 'Farrall's likely to have Ike Goldfink with him. If he decides to do some lookin', that lanky saloonist's got Crow blood in him, he'll stick to your tail like a burr to a cowhide.'

But the words were lost on Joel Cramer, a laconic warning without the power to interrupt black thoughts that were looking ahead and, once again, already beset by niggling doubts. Sure, Lawson's dying words had been plain enough, and he had no reason to lie. But as Cramer urged his horse up the east bank of Jackson's Creek, he knew that something in what the killer had told him didn't ring true.

★ ★ ★

The plaintive notes of the harmonica, played with skill and feeling by Jak La Roche, brought the sadness welling up in Joel Cramer. The tune was 'When Johnny Comes Marching Home Again', its poignant message haunting and painful. The man called Tucson had spread his blankets on a bed of dead leaves, for a pillow had placed his saddle against the bole of a tree. In the light of the flickering campfire he was lying back and looking across the small clearing at the gambler through eyes blurred with unshed tears. He swallowed hard, failed to shift the painful lump in his throat and with fingers that trembled began to roll a cigarette.

'Cut that out before you charm those damn Comanches out of the trees,' he said huskily, and La Roche's blue eyes danced in the firelight as he finished what he was playing, tapped the battered instrument against his thigh and stowed it away in his shirt pocket.

He was sitting cross-legged with the light of the flames playing on the flat planes of his face, an imp-like figure seen hazily through the rising smoke. His check jacket hung alongside him on a branch he'd driven into the earth; his pistol lay on a flat stone within reach of his right hand. He bent forward without straightening his legs, tipped coffee into a cup from the blackened pot hanging on a forked stick over the flames, took time tasting the dark liquid as his eyes became thoughtful.

'I guess that tune touched a raw nerve, and told me your boy's name,' he said perceptively. 'But if them Comanche have got him, bringin' them out of the trees to chew the rag is surely what you want?'

'At a time of my choosing.'

'What about Farrall?'

Cramer licked the paper, crimped the cigarette, looked at his handiwork.

'What about him?'

'I warned you about Goldfink. You already know Farrall's bein' driven hard. What you've got to ask yourself while you're settin' there is, how far's he prepared to go and who's doin' the pushin'?'

The match flared, brighter than the dying campfire and, Cramer decided, a whole lot brighter than his thinking. He'd left the burnt out ruins of his soddy convinced that Lawson and Wood had carried out the killing and kidnapping on Dyke Manson's orders, and nothing that had happened in Jackson's Bend had changed that opinion. But at Pueblo it had been clear that Manson was ignorant of the two gunslingers' whereabouts. All right, so riding along with Theaker had paid dividends, and got rid of the killers, but if Manson wasn't the man behind that crime, who was?

Maybe Wood had been telling the truth, and the Comanche were holding his boy. But that suggested Lawson and Wood had been working on their own, which in turn raised questions about Butch Farrall's ruthless attempts to drive Cramer out of town . . . and the rider who'd called at the jail with a message that turned up the heat.

But why should any of that concern him? His one aim was to locate his boy. The first indication that he was getting close had come from the dead killer. Mysterious riders and crazy lawmen were no more of a nuisance than flies buzzing around a steer's head: something to be brushed off, then ignored until the next time they came too close.

'It ain't unheard of,' La Roche said, breaking into his confused train of thought, 'for a crooked lawman to be in cahoots with the chief of a roving band of Injuns. And if, in addition, that lawman's got a lucrative sideline goin' supplying corn whiskey to those Injuns, it'd be in his interests to keep everything under his hat.'

Cramer blew a jet of smoke towards the fire, watched it drift into the heat thrown out by the glowing logs and rise sharply towards the dark trees where a canopy of wet leaves filtered the light of the high-floating moon.

'Corn whiskey from where?'

115

'I guess you was only lookin' for one thing.'

'At Pueblo?'

'Where else? There was something weird ashinin' in that big barn when we rode in. Later, during that spell on the gallery, Manson glanced over that way lookin' kinda worried.'

'If Dyke Manson's runnin' a still with Farrall sellin' the moonshine to the redskins, that means Lawson and Wood were dealin' with the Comanche on their own: two separate factions doin' two different deals with those Indians.' Cramer shook his head in disbelief. 'Hell, they'd've been treadin' on each other's toes.'

'Why separate them? Butch Farrall could be behind both deals. If he is, that's two darn good reasons he's got for huntin' you down.'

The coffee cup rattled as La Roche set it on the flat stone alongside his pistol. He picked up a green stick, poked the logs until they collapsed and tilted his head to watch the sparks soar then wink out against the canopy of wet leaves.

'All right,' Cramer said, leaving it at that, knowing what he'd heard smacked of the truth but left the question of the mystery rider unanswered. 'I guess that problem's plumb talked out until sun-up — which brings us to you, La Roche, and your part in this.'

From across the fire the little gambler smiled. 'If the way I set that pistol all loaded up and ready has got you worried, then forget it. That's for Farrall, not you, just in case he decides sun-up's too long to wait.'

'That's not what I meant. Your whole damn involvement in this don't make sense. And now you're makin' it worse because you're still watchin' my back, protectin' me — at considerable risk to yourself — for some reason I can't fathom.'

'I'm a poor Louisiana boy, Tucson, born small, came out the womb shufflin' a deck of cards with uncanny skill. But Louisiana was old and tired when I grew up, and after the War we drifted West, workin' the saloons in harbour towns reekin' of fish, all the way along the Gulf until we hit the Bravo. Wasn't too long after that . . . ' he chuckled softly. 'What do we call it, Tucson? The night of the long guns? Well, on that night in Nuevo Laredo our lives got all tangled up in a way you haven't yet tumbled to but, when you do, you'll know why I'm here now.'

'We?'

'Huh?'

'You said *we* moved West.'

'Yeah, so I did,' La Roche said — then turned his head sharply, a hand upraised in warning as out in the woods a twig snapped.

Cramer was already up, flicking away the cigarette as he rolled swiftly off his blankets and sprang to his feet. He took a long stride, scooped up two handfuls of damp earth and dumped it on the fire, rattling the coffee pot. The ruddy glow expired with a dying hiss. White smoke drifted high. Darkness closed in on the clearing.

Cramer drew his six-gun.

La Roche had already melted away. The clearing was a shallow basin. Their hobbled horses were dozing at the edge of the encircling trees. Cramer approached them, rested a hand reassuringly on his own mount's warm neck. As it lifted its head, nuzzled him wetly, Cramer slipped past into the woods and went still.

He sniffed, smelling only the horses, wet undergrowth, the sharp tang of the smoke haze hanging like night mist above the dead fire. His eardrums ached, but picked up no sounds. La Roche had faded away into the darkness. Whoever or whatever had snapped the dead branch had gone to ground.

For five long minutes, Cramer stayed frozen. Gradually, his straining eyes grew accustomed to the faint, filtered moonlight. In the maze of tree trunks and tangled branches, shadows began to move. He tensed, squeezed his eyes shut, opened them — and the shadows were still. The air enveloped him, wrapping him in its chill. He shivered, then started in fright as, behind him, one of the horses snorted in sleep.

Cramer drew in a slow breath, let it out. Still nothing; no sound, no movement — and he knew that was because Butch Farrall and the Crow tracker who ran a saloon in his spare time were beyond the cottonwoods on the far bank of Jackson's Creek, snoring in their warm blankets. He stepped back against his mount's flank, felt the living heat begin to soak through his shirt, turned to duck under the animal's neck — and immediately stiffened and went still.

In the clearing, close to the campfire's blackened embers, a man crouched.

Behind Cramer, the horse moved restlessly. He reached up, soothed it, lifted his six-gun. The sound as he cocked it was clear and sharp. The indistinct shape by the fire didn't move.

Cramer stepped away from the trees, began to move down the slope into the hollow, called loudly, 'Hold it right there, feller . . . '

And from the other side of the clearing, Jak La Roche said, 'What you aimin' to do, Tucson — plug a hole in my best check jacket?'

9

They spent a restless night and moved off shortly after dawn having eaten a cold breakfast of tough jerky washed down with clear spring water. Once they were out of the trees the ground sloped in flat planes towards the river and, as the fresh horses stretched out in an easy lope, they were again like ghosts floating on mist that lifted off Jackson's Creek to cloak the open grassland. But the clouds that had brought the night's rain had dispersed. The brilliant sun was already warm and, as they rode steadily northwards along the banks of the creek, that pleasant warmth promised to turn into the scorching heat of a Kansas summer.

An hour later Cramer became uncomfortably aware that the blood-stained shirt he wore was acquiring a ripe, fetid odour. The sun had risen high, and was beginning to heat up the filthy garment. With a grunt he dipped his head to his shoulder and took a deep sniff of blood, dirt and sweat, screwed up his nose in disgust, then looked up to see La Roche grinning across at him.

'If them Injuns don't get you,' the gambler said, 'you'll die of a fever from them poisonous fumes.'

'Or a bullet in the back,' Cramer said, and saw the smile fade from La Roche's face as he twisted to glance over his shoulder.

'You seen something I ain't?'

'Been keepin' my eye on them for some time. Two riders. Some way back, but closing. Right now they're hidden behind that last rise.'

'Goddamn!' The gambler reined in hard, spun his horse in a flurry of dust to look back down the trail. As Cramer came alongside he said, 'I warned you about Farrall, and now I'm beginnin' to get a real bad feeling.'

'Matches the one I've had ever since

I rode into town.'

'Yeah, that's understandable — but, later, did you notice there was no reception committee when we rode up to Dyke Manson's?'

Cramer nodded. 'So?'

'So, that rider I saw leavin' town went somewhere. If not Pueblo, then where?'

They had reached an area where the water tumbled over rocks at a shallow ford, and the land falling towards the creek was a maze of grassy ridges split by hollows in which trees clustered alongside dry winter run-offs. The high ridge they had crossed was two miles back, its crest already shimmering in the heat. Watching it for sign of movement, eyes narrowed against the glare, Cramer said, 'Only place I can think of he could've been makin' for is an Indian encampment somewhere along the creek — and a bunch of whoopin' Comanche braves is tough enough to face without them havin' prior warning, if that's what you're suggestin'. If you are, it could be we're caught between them and Farrall — if that is Farrall back there.'

'A lot of ifs in there,' La Roche said with dry humour as he slid from the saddle, 'but, yeah, that's roughly in line with my thinkin'.'

Cramer took his eyes off the ridge, then also climbed down and let his horse wander a few yards with trailing reins to graze.

'Well, now's as good a time as any if you want to cut and run,' he said. The little gambler's gaudy jacket was open wide and flung back clear of his hips. His pistol jutted from his belt.

'Right,' La Roche said. His blue eyes were guarded, his body tense but his small hands hanging loose.

'Unless,' Cramer said, 'you've got something to say about that move from Louisiana made by you and someone you didn't name. And a feller you saved from a bunch of *Rurales*, only to find out, too late, they wanted him for killin' ... who was that tinhorn I killed, La Roche?'

'My brother,' La Roche said, and though Cramer had been expecting an answer along those lines, still the shock hit him hard. There was the glitter of steel in the gambler's blue eyes, a coldness, Cramer reckoned, that could be interpreted as hate. 'Older than me by twelve years,' La Roche went on. 'Made him close to thirty when he took a fatal slug — and now you're gonna tell me he was dealin' off the bottom, palmin' aces or some such.'

'He was cheating. You were his kid brother; you know I'm right.'

The bald statement was made in a tone that brooked no argument, and suddenly La Roche's whole body relaxed and his grin became wide and genuine. 'Other than you, I don't see any witnesses around, so why don't we chew this one over some other time, Tucson, when you've got less pressing problems?'

'Now that I know the real reason you're ridin' with me,' Joel Cramer said wryly, 'that would be like me bein' surrounded by them Comanche, Farrall and Goldfink ridin' down the hill, then discoverin' there's a live scorpion sleepin' inside my shirt.'

'No self respectin' scorpion,' La Roche said, 'would go near that bloodstained rag,' and suddenly both men were grinning and, to Cramer, there came the realization that in the rare times he had smiled with genuine good humour in the past twenty-four hours, it had been in the company of this man.

Yet if he had killed Jak La Roche's brother in Laredo, then the little gambler was along not for the ride, but for revenge. The hate he had just seen blazing like cold fire in the little man's eyes made that a certainty, but if he intended to kill Cramer, why was he biding his time?

'I told you,' La Roche said, once again, to Cramer's chagrin, appearing to read his thoughts, 'we'll talk about my brother's death some other time

— like, when we've dealt with those two fellers who, right now, are comin' hell-for-leather over that rise.'

Without waiting for Cramer's answer he strode to his horse, slipped his Winchester out of its saddle-boot, rammed it into his shoulder and leaned across his horse to use the saddle as a rest as he fired three carefully aimed shots at the distant riders.

'And that,' Cramer said, watching the careering horsemen sheer away from the puffs of dust as the shots echoed flatly, 'could put us in deep trouble if them Comanche have been waitin' on a prearranged signal.'

'Hell,' La Roche said disgustedly, 'is this the man was as cool as ice facin' them *Rurales*? Did Tucson Joel Cramer build a reputation by gettin' the jitters when hot lead starts flyin'?'

Cramer smiled grimly. 'A man loses everything he's got it hits hard, La Roche, changes his whole outlook on life. But you're right: only a fool'd worry about Indians at his back when

128

he's faced by two men intent on blastin' him into perdition.'

'And pretty damn soon, at that.'

There was a tightness in La Roche's voice that drove all the senseless self-pity out of Cramer and sent him across to his horse to collect his rifle. The gambler snapped another shot, then swore softly as again it went wide.

Cramer jacked a shell into the Winchester's breech and lifted it to his shoulder, but, close enough now to be recognizable, the hot sun at their backs, Butch Farrall and Ike Goldfink had suddenly realized their danger and split up. Rifles flashed in the sunlight as they held them high and hammered their broncs in wide arcs that saw them dipping out of sight in the irregular terrain. At once, the drum of pounding hooves gave way to a silence that was oppressive and set taut nerves jangling. A haze of yellow dust drifted in the sun-drenched stillness.

'Looks like Goldfink'll come along the creek,' Cramer said softly. 'Farrall's workin' his way around, aimin' to come at us down one of them gullies.'

'Need to be this one, if he's gonna get close,' La Roche said, with a jerk of his head indicating the nearest dry wash. 'Either way, we'd be fools to hang around in the open.' And moving with a haste that matched the urgency of his words, he swung into the saddle and spun his horse away from the creek.

Cramer watched him head fast up the run-off, hooves rattling on loose stones as he rode hard for fifty yards before pulling into a stand of stunted trees that was between him and the high end of the gully.

Puzzled yet again by the actions of the little gambler, who by rights should have been exacting revenge but seemed determined to save his life, Cramer shook his head in exasperation then stepped up into the saddle and swung his own horse back towards the creek.

As he did so he heard the soft pounding of hooves. A horse was approaching fast, following the course of the water but hidden by a low bluff. Swiftly, Cramer looked all around him for cover. There was none. And now the rider was close.

What the hell was going on? Had Farrall decided to come in with guns blazing, leaving the lanky Crow saloonist to take them from the flank?

With a muttered curse, Cramer cast a swift glance up the dry wash to where La Roche's horse was walking away from the stand of gnarled trees, then again flung himself from the saddle and smacked his horse on the rump. It tossed its head and trotted away up the gully and, rifle in hand, Cramer ran fast up a short grassy slope.

The galloping horse was close, too close, the sound of hooves now an ominous, insistent drumming. At the crest of the rise, Cramer hit the hard ground and snatched off his Stetson. Breathing hard, he inched forward on his belly until he could look south down the broad, glittering stretch of Jackson's Creek.

The horse was riderless.

Cramer took in the flashing hooves and flapping stirrups, the flowing mane, the slick, empty saddle — then clenched his teeth and threw himself to the side. As he did so a rifle cracked from the ridge above the dry wash. With a solid thump the slug drilled into the grass where Cramer had been lying. As he rolled, hanging onto the rifle and tumbling down the slope, a second shot followed the first and he felt the icy brush of death as the bullet touched his hair.

Then a second rifle opened up, pumping away from the high end of the wash: Ike Goldfink had entered the fray.

But now Cramer's desperate roll had carried him to the bottom of the slope. He swung his body around, straightened his legs and dug in his heels. Momentum threw him up onto his feet. Still out in the open, dangerously exposed, he turned fast and fell into a crouch. As he swung around, rifle at his hip, he snapped a wild shot and levered another bullet into the breech. His eyes raked the ridge. A dark shape moved on the skyline. Sunlight glinted on metal. Cramer leaped sideways as muzzle flame winked dimly against the glare of the hot sun. Alongside his ear the deadly bullet hummed wickedly. Then his Winchester was at his shoulder. His second shot cracked. A dark hat flapped high like a startled, soaring raven. From the ridge there was a roar of pain, or anger.

And for a long moment, Marshal Butch Farrall's rifle was silent.

In every tight spot he'd been in — and there had been so many over the years that he'd long ago given up counting — Cramer had always figured that a man who went on the attack when by rights he was as good as dead deserved to come out top of the heap. Whether he did or not depended on who the fickle gods favoured, and how rattled the opponent got when he saw the man he thought he'd got pinned down charging like a madman straight at a couple of blazing pistols.

Well, Cramer's first slug had whipped Farrall's grubby Stetson clean off his greasy hair, but if the bullet had drilled through the hat without inflicting damage on the hard skull beneath, the marshal wasn't going to stay lying down for too long. And with the fierce rattle of gunfire further up the dry wash telling Cramer that Jak La Roche was keeping the lanky saloonist occupied, he decided somewhat ruefully that he was in yet another of those situations where his theory was going to be put to the test.

Ruefully, because losing count of the times he'd tried, and the times he'd come out on top, still left him at the mercy of the law of averages. About which, Cramer reckoned with a faint grin, La Roche, the gambler, would no doubt enlighten him.

But not now.

What seemed to Cramer like a whole hatful of jumbled thinking had passed in the blink of an eye; the time it took for the brutal gunman on the ridge to die hard — or pull himself together. A snatched glance brought Cramer bad news: the marshal was still a fighting force, for his dark bulk was back in position, the shiny rifle already swinging back into line. Another quick glance up the wash where only the soft whinny of a horse broke an uneasy silence and he picked out the lean form of Ike Goldfink, on foot and in shadow, edging towards the grove of stunted trees with his back to a low rock outcrop, unseen by La Roche.

'Watch to your right, gambler!' roared Cramer. Then, jaw clamped, Winchester tossed aside like a useless stick and his cocked six gun in his fist, he set out to put his time-worn philosophy to the ultimate test.

Cramer cut at an angle across the rake of the slope down which he'd so recently tumbled, spurs chinking as he ran hard for the higher ridge, breath rasping in his throat as he fought to take a weaving route on ground that was uneven and treacherous underfoot.

A coarse laugh rang out as Farrall caught on to Cramer's bold play and hoisted his bulk high the better to see. He'd spent the seconds Cramer lost to thought ducked down and thumbing slugs into the rifle. Now, bullets pocked the dirt under Cramer's stumbling feet as, in his eagerness, the marshal overcompensated for the downhill shots and blasted a fast fusillade that was too low by far.

But Cramer was rapidly running out of steam. An iron band clamped his heaving chest. His thigh muscles burned, his arms were dragging lead weights. He strained his neck to look up, saw the marshal looming over him, standing spread-legged and unassailable atop the final, jutting overhang. Again that coarse laugh rang out, washing over Cramer as if to mock the uselessness of a battle-plan that had run its course, and failed.

The overhang was an impossible barrier. The long way round gave the advantage to Farrall — where, Cramer thought bitterly, it had lain from the outset. Above him, the hot steel of Farrall's Winchester rattled as the slug that bore Cramer's name and would rip him apart was slammed home. And there were now no options, for the slope had beaten Cramer. His last upward stride was a trembling excuse for a bold advance. He halted, swaying, fell forward against the steep slope to clutch the coarse grass with his fingers as he blinked away tears drawn by the stinging salt of his sweat.

The last time he had blinked away tears they had been tears of grief as, on a storm-swept ridge, he dug a lonely grave. The last time he had felt despair was when a screaming child had been carried away into the black night.

. . . *the only thing he could do for his wife now that she was gone was to find her boy and bring him home . . . a man who goes on the attack when by rights he's as good as dead deserves to come out top of the heap.*

And as his heart thundered and the gorge rose within him at the prospect of failure, Joel Cramer gathered his strength and rose up to fling himself at the overhang and let loose with a wild yell that rocked the marshal back on his heels and sent the shot that had been intended for Cramer winging harmlessly towards the searing skies.

Cramer slammed an elbow over the lip. His clawed fingers dug into grass and soft earth. His boots scrabbled for a foothold. The earth began to crumble. Inexorably, his clinging fingers were loosened and dragged backwards by his weight. He clamped his jaw, breath hissing through his nostrils, brought the heavy pistol over in a wide chopping, flailing motion. The violent motion stopped the slide.

But now, Butch Farrall had recovered.

Eyes narrowed, Cramer stared up at the marshal, saw the veins distended in the man's thick neck as his heavy right hand worked the Winchester's lever.

The rifle came down. The gaping muzzle settled, just three feet from Cramer's pale, sweating countenance.

But the wild swing with his free right arm had assisted the cocking of his pistol. As its weight whipped down the heel of his thumb snapped back the hammer. His forefinger was already bone-white, squeezing the trigger. The pistol levelled. The hammer slipped from beneath his thumb.

The blast of the big .45 drove his hand upwards, tore his fingers loose from the crumbling soil. As he slipped backwards he saw blood blossom on the marshal's shirt front, saw the rifle slip from nerveless fingers, saw the thick legs crumple beneath the big man's dead weight.

Then Cramer was falling backwards as a chunk of the overhang broke away. He landed heavily on his shoulders in a shower of rocks and soil, felt his teeth snap shut as he allowed his bent legs to swing over in a 360° backward roll that brought him up on his feet but fighting for balance. He half fell, half turned, tripped over his own feet and allowed momentum to carry him down the slope at a jog.

Elation washed over him. It was over. The fickle gods had come down on the side of good, not evil. The philosophy that had seen him through countless dangerous scrapes was still being smiled on by Lady Luck, the law of averages still working in his favour.

The hunt for his boy was still on.

At the bottom of the slope he saw La Roche leading both horses down the wash. The lathered riderless horse — Farrall's, Cramer surmised — had turned away from the creek and now, head high and to one side to lift the trailing reins, trotted across towards La Roche and the two broncs.

Cramer collected his rifle, went to meet the little gambler.

'Goldfink?'

'Dead.' La Roche indicated the ridge.

'But that feller won't lie down.'

Butch Farrall was lumbering drunkenly down the slope. Sunlight caught the slick blood on his shirt, the sweat beading his brow, the lank, greasy hair. His eyes were narrowed with pain. As he drew near he seemed to see Cramer and La Roche for the first time and veered sharply away, making for his horse.

'Farrall!'

The lawman stopped, swaying. As Cramer approached, Farrall spat, staining the grass red. His hand reached out, fumbled for his horse's reins.

'Who put you up to this?'

The grin was ferocious, challenging, revealing ugly, bloodstained teeth. 'The authorities,' Farrall said, his voice tight with agony. 'You're Tucson Joel Cramer, wanted by the law.'

'What about Wood, Lawson?'

'Names,' Farrall said. He heaved himself awkwardly into the saddle, emitting a gasping groan as he clung to the horn. 'You plucked 'em out of your hat, used 'em for an excuse to go after Manson.'

'But you say Manson's not involved.'

It was a statement that required no answer. Farrall let the words fall unheeded, spat again, said, 'If your boy's been took by Injuns — '

'Why Indians?' Cramer cut in. 'It was white men came to my soddy. Are you saying they handed the boy over?'

'If you're lookin' for confirmation, I can't give it,' Farrall said, his face pasty as he gathered the reins, kneed the horse around. 'But if, if there was a Lawson and Wood, and if, like you say, Manson ain't involved — what the hell would two grown men be doin' snatchin' a slip of a boy from a man who couldn't afford to pay no ransom?'

He clicked wetly, jabbed with his spurs and set off for Jackson's Creek at a jolting trot that threatened to unseat him. They watched him swaying as he clung to the horn, saw the horse negotiate the steep bank and send a spray of glistening droplets high in the air as it splashed into the water, listened to the flat clacking of stones as the creek was crossed.

'Headin' the wrong way,' Jak La Roche said, and Cramer watched Butch Farrall turn the dripping horse away from town and point it in a north-westerly direction.

'Maybe that's for the best. I've only got a dying man's word for it that my boy's with the Comanche. For some reason, Farrall's bein' devious. If this . . . this thing with the Injuns don't show colour, the truth maybe lies in that man's stubborn head.'

'I seem to recall tellin' you sooner or later you'd need to find out who's pushin' him,' La Roche said. 'I guess this means you ain't any closer to gettin' rid of that shirt.'

Cramer stretched to ease a crick in his neck, and grinned. 'About as close as you are to usin' that pistol on the man who killed your brother.'

'Jesus!' La Roche said soulfully. 'And you call Farrall devious.' He gazed across the river to where cottonwoods shimmered in the heat; seemed, to Cramer, to hesitate, then said quietly, 'My brother's name was Pierre. Like I said, we moved west from Louisiana . . .'

Cramer shook his head. 'I shot a man dead in a bar in Nuevo Laredo, a gambler, pullin' aces out of every damn place except his lyin' mouth — but he didn't go by the name of Pierre.'

When he turned away from La Roche with a puzzled frown, his eyes were drawn to the far distance and he said, softly, but with a quiver of excitement in his voice, 'Don't look now, but we've got company.'

Five hundred yards away, two motionless, mounted Comanche were silhouetted on the skyline.

10

'All right,' Cramer said. 'I've found them renegade Indians — now what the hell do I do?'

'Follow 'em, if you want to find your boy,' La Roche said. 'But easy does it.'

'Can I trust a Louisiana man when it comes to the Comanche?'

'They any different from Creeks, or Cherokee?'

Baffled, Cramer shook his head. 'I'm askin' out of ignorance, not wisdom. I've gotta confess, ridin' into a redskin camp ain't the brightest idea I've had.'

They mounted up and spurred away from the creek, covering the 500 yards or so to the high ground at an easy lope in the hope that if they showed no aggression they would be able to talk with the Comanche. But long before they reached and crested the rise the Indians had melted away into the shimmering landscape and, though the two men spent long minutes squinting into the distance through eyes shaded by their tugged-down Stetsons, they could pick out no movement on the sun-baked plains.

'Now what?'

La Roche grinned. 'I already told you: follow them.'

'You're a barrel of laughs, gambler.'

'They didn't go thataway,' La Roche reasoned, hooking his thumb over his shoulder. 'Land slopes to the water, so we would've seen them if they cut west towards the creek. If they'd headed east, that'd be away from water, which don't make any sense.'

Cramer grunted his doubt. 'You see their dust to the north?'

'I don't see dust anywhere I look,' La Roche said, 'but we sure as hell can't sit here all day chewin' the fat.' He eased his weight in the saddle, cocked his head to look sideways at Cramer. 'Why is it I get the impression you're arguin' *against* goin' after them?'

'Because I'm scared, that's why,' Cramer said gruffly. 'Not scared of a bunch of Comanche braves — hell, a man holdin' a weapon's the same, white or red — I guess I'm scared of what I might find when I finally catch up with them.'

'Or might not,' La Roche said astutely. He nodded understanding, said quietly, 'You're a bodacious man, Tucson, and, yeah, that's the Louisiana in me a-talkin'. Then, without waiting for further comment, he clicked his tongue and set off down the slope.

They followed the Comanche blind, catching only occasional glimpses of the Indians that came, Cramer admitted grudgingly, not from the braves' carelessness, but from their indifference and scorn; and all the while he and La Roche suffered under a blazing sun that took its own sweet time searing a path across awesome blue skies, crossing its zenith and starting on the long slow swoop that would drag night over the land like a dark blanket. Already, in its wake, heavy clouds were gathering, but they were distant in both miles and time, and if they did pose a threat then it was something within Cramer's understanding.

The same could not be said for all that had transpired in the thirty-six hours since the killing of his brave, beautiful wife. In that time it seemed that nothing had made sense. With Dyke Manson the name planted in his mind by the 'breed's earlier visit to the soddy, at the outset there had been the clear aim to recruit the help of Jackson's Bend's lawman and set out to rescue his boy. But in Butch Farrall he had found a beast of a man driven by his own crude ambitions, hounded by an unseen, powerful force. When, at Dyke Manson's decaying Pueblo, there had been no sign of his boy or the killers . . . well, just about then everything seemed to fall apart.

With hindsight, he should have confronted the 'breed, asked blunt questions instead of listening to bunkhouse gossip. But, also with the benefit of hindsight, he knew that he had done the best he could in the circumstances. The raid on Dan Packham's soddy had led him first to Wood, then to Lawson. The dying man's story of handing the boy to the Comanche was credible, because for weeks Cramer had been worried about Quanah Parker's braves — and Jak La Roche had heard those same disturbing rumours in Ike Goldfink's saloon, and had been able to add his own thoughts on whisky peddling and the possibility of the devious marshal's deep involvement in more than one lawless scheme.

Still and all . . .

Why give the boy to the Comanche?

And what if he was obsessed with Dyke Manson to the exclusion of all else? A man could stick stubbornly, blindly to the one track when clear signs were pointing in another direction. Names had been mentioned twice, once by Farrall in his office, once by Ike Goldfink when he'd replied to a question, but on each occasion Cramer had let them slide past like logs drifting downstream.

'Smoke, some ways ahead.'

The gambler's sudden sharp words broke through Cramer's thoughts, snapping his gaze to the way ahead.

Like the earlier river mist that had been dissipated by the sun, the smoke from the Indian encampment was flattened by the oppressive heat and hung low and white. But it was drifting, and thinner than mist, and through it, like the ghosts of distant mountain peaks, poked the tops of maybe a dozen tipis.

At the edge of the smoke, motionless, naked skin glistening in the bright sunshine, the two horsemen who had with indifference led them this far awaited their approach. The two Comanche carried short lances. They wore breech-clouts and beaded moccasins. Their legs hung loose.

'No warpaint,' Cramer said as they drew near.

'A few daubs of paint looks scary but never killed no one,' La Roche pointed out, and Cramer flashed him a grin that was stiff, and forced. He was very close to an answer, he felt it in his bones. But the raw fear at what that answer might be was like a sickness leaching the strength from his body and soul.

'You speak the Comanche lingo?'

'Hell,' La Roche said with a nervous grin, 'I reckon I have more than enough trouble speakin' English.'

As they drew near, the smoke became a thin veil through which the Indian village could be seen clearly, lazing in the heat of the day. A few squaws had emerged from the tipis, others were making their way across the grass from the creek carrying bundles of wet clothes. From the horse herd picketed in a grove of trees to the east of the village, three more braves came racing around the perimeter to join the two already awaiting the white men. They

151

rode recklessly, deliberately vainglorious as they brandished lances and war shields, arrived in a billowing cloud of dust and gave vent to drawn-out, ululating cries as they spun the ponies in tight circles before jerking them to a halt.

Together, they formed a half-circle, barring the way into the village. Behind them, Cramer noted with a sudden quickening of the pulse, restrained only by the sharp cries of the squaws, curious, naked children were scampering towards the village's edge.

The tension was palpable.

'That one,' La Roche said softly, indicating with a slight movement of his head the tall brave who was now at the centre of a group of five. 'They're deferring to him, so I guess he's top dog.'

Twenty paces from the waiting Indians, Cramer drew rein. Spurs chinked musically as he let his horse step sideways, distancing himself from La Roche.

The tall Indian in the centre of the group said something in a deep, resonant voice. Another Indian laughed. A third spun his horse and rode a short distance away, then came racing back to swing in and ride at a thunderous gallop behind the two white men. Again he spun his horse on the hard, dry earth, and suddenly Cramer was engulfed in choking dust and felt the heat of the man and his pony, felt his nostrils flare to alien scents as the naked Indian leaned close and touched his shoulder with a hard hand.

Then the brave was gone. He rejoined the group, dark eyes flashing with triumph, and behind the now openly grinning Indians a group of young boys, all about ten years old, were jumping up and down and giggling with excitement. Then one of them broke away. Slapping his rump as if he were on horseback, he skilfully mimed the actions of the Indian who had counted coup on Cramer as he ran in a tight circle, back into the cluster of tipis. As Cramer watched, the youngster spun his imaginary pony, naked feet kicking up dust as he sprang high to touch the shoulder of a baby held in the arms of one of the squaws.

And suddenly, Cramer's heart was hammering in his throat. The mimicry had been frighteningly exact, the victim carefully chosen to match Cramer. The baby on whom the boy had ceremoniously counted coup had blond hair; the infant had clearly been born of a white woman and, in that instant, Tucson Joel Cramer knew that he had found his son.

11

'You see what I see?'

'Goddammit!' Cramer said huskily. 'It's him.'

'Easy, now, easy,' La Roche said.

He kneed his horse forward, walked it across the narrow patch of dusty ground and drew to a halt in front of the tall Indian's horse. Then he lifted his hand in greeting, and to Cramer's confusion he began to talk to the Indian in soft, guttural tones that at first brought a thin smile of appreciation to the brave's greased, high-cheek-boned countenance, then for some reason caused the glittering black eyes to narrow.

But how do you concentrate when the boy you had thought lost forever — and, yes, for the first time Cramer allowed that thought to enter his mind — is being carried away from you in the arms of a dusky Indian squaw, and the shrill cries of the boys who had brought him to your notice are like the frenzied yapping of a pack of hunting dogs, snapping at the woman's naked heels.

Involuntarily, Cramer touched his horse with his spurs, the mild bite of the sharp rowels urging it forwards. His eyes were lifted, looking beyond the menacing half-circle of Indian braves. Peering anxiously between those muscular, naked forms he could see the dust kicked up by the bare feet of the children drifting to mingle with the hanging smoke of the campfires. The scampering youngsters weaved a dizzy pattern of glistening brown skin and black hair, racing hither and yon with flashing grins as the squaw shuffled on through the encampment, oblivious to their play.

Then Cramer was brought up short. A harsh command snapped through his thoughts. A lance whipped down, its shaft whacking his upper thighs as it cracked down across the saddle.

Urged on by the spurs, his horse had carried him into the half-circle formed by the five braves and had begun to force a way through. Still squinting into the dust and smoke, Cramer cursed softly. Automatically, his gloved hand reached down to grasp the lance's shaft. He lifted it, twisted up and back, and was immediately jolted off balance as a snorting pony crowded him from the other side and a sinewy hand slapped his chest and fastened on the front of his stiffened, bloody shirt.

'It ain't him, Tucson!'

Cramer blinked.

'You hear me!'

La Roche's voice was urgent, compelling. Frowning, Cramer looked around for the little Louisiana gambler, saw him, and cuffed the Indian's hand from his shirt, heard the young brave's amused chuckle as he relinquished his hold and let his pony dance away. Then the lance was wrenched from Cramer's grasp and as that brave, too, whirled away from him, Cramer let his horse

157

walk backwards, easing away from the unbroken line.

'There is a white boy,' La Roche said, his voice deliberately placating but with an undercurrent suggesting there was more to come. He's giving me the good news, Cramer thought, withholding the bad because he's scared I'll go crazy.

He shook his head angrily, walked his horse to where the gambler was slouched in the saddle as he confronted the tall brave.

'I've got eyes to see with,' he said. 'Is that the best you can do, ask questions when the answer's already plain as daylight?'

'If you've got eyes,' La Roche said, 'you can see that kid's at home. He's been here close on a year, Tucson, forgot all about life with white men.'

'He told you that?' Cramer looked into the tall brave's black, fathomless eyes and said softly, 'He's lying — or you heard wrong.'

La Roche made a soft exclamation of annoyance. 'There's five lances could

158

stick us before we moved a dozen yards, a score of eager braves back there with stolen army carbines. They're not threatened, Tucson — so why would he lie?'

'All right. Tell him I want to see the boy, close up.'

'That's as good as *callin'* him a liar.'

'Tell him!'

La Roche shrugged nervously. 'Just make damn sure you're ready to turn tail, get the hell out of here, because I'd wager a fistful of double eagles on this big buck turnin' nasty.'

When he began talking to the tall brave La Roche stumbled over the unfamiliar words. He had started to sweat, and had come up out of his slouch and turned in the saddle so that his hand could leap to the six-gun poked through his belt. Cramer watched the brave's eyes, then shifted impatiently in the saddle and set leather creaking and spurs chinking as he stood in the stirrups to stare anxiously into the village. The squaw holding the white boy had paused in her leisurely stroll, and was talking to a group of women. Village gossip, he thought, and gritted his teeth. Laughter tinkled as dusky faces turned towards him. The women's eyes sparkled in the sun like dark, lustrous jewels.

Cramer felt a sickness in his stomach as he looked at the tiny, tow-headed figure in the squaw's arms. La Roche's words stumbled on as the other braves moved restlessly on their ragged ponies, yet it had now become clear to Cramer that the little gambler was wasting his time. He'd always suspected there had been something cock-eyed in the notion that Wood and Lawson had handed his boy over to the Comanche, but until now the reason why had eluded him. Well, the little gambler might wager a fistful of double eagles on the big buck turning nasty, but that Comanche would never have handed gold coins to Wood and Lawson — always supposing he had any — in exchange for something he

160

was accustomed to taking by force.

But somebody had paid Wood and Lawson. According to Manson's gunman, Gittins, the two men Cramer was hunting rode into Pueblo with a silver dollar but a matter of days later were playing poker with double eagles.

Payment in advance, then — but for what, and from whom? And where, in God's name, was his boy!

There was an emptiness like an unnatural hunger eating away at Cramer's soul.

Again La Roche's sharp call broke through his desolation and, as he turned to the little gambler, he saw the big buck swinging his pony to issue an order to one of the braves.

'You're lucky,' La Roche called. 'Instead of stickin' you with that lance, he's decided to humour you.'

'Tell him to forget it.'

'Jesus!'

'Hey, feller!'

The big brave's head snapped around at Cramer's shout, his single heavy plait studded with silver conchos swinging across his bronze shoulder.

'Where from?' Cramer pointed to the white boy, spread his hands, palms up, contrived to look puzzled. 'Where did you get the white boy?'

'You think he'll tell you?'

'They're not threatened, remember? This is a renegade bunch, split from Quanah Parker's main band. Renegades are convinced they're untouchable, so he'll do some bragging.'

'Yeah,' La Roche said. 'But don't expect him to give nothing away.'

Cramer's pantomime had amused the brave. He turned to his companions, aped Cramer's actions in a startling imitation of baffled incomprehension, then tilted his head back and roared with laughter. Then, abruptly, the laughter ceased. Just as the other brave had done, he kicked his pony into a gallop, but instead of circling he rode it hard and fast at Cramer, only hauling it back at the last instant into a sat-back, rearing halt that brought him face to face with Cramer in a flurry of pawing hooves and a cloud of settling dust. The pony snorted and stamped, nostrils flaring. The brave's eyes swept over Cramer with arrogant disdain, staring with open contempt at the filthy shirt encrusted with dried blood, the lean face drawn by weariness and strain.

Suddenly, the erect lance dipped. Cramer's horse backed nervously, stopped, trembling, as Cramer tightened his knees. The lance touched his thigh, slid, settled on the booted Winchester.

'That's what he wants,' La Roche said.

'Tell him it's his if he comes up with the right answer.'

'That ain't something you can judge, one way or the other.'

'He'll confirm what I've already half figured out — so do it.'

La Roche spoke slowly. As the brave listened, his dark eyes gleamed. He looked at Cramer's Winchester, pulled his eyes away. When he spoke, there was no need for La Roche to translate.

'Blue . . . Stack,' the brave said ponderously, and he moved his sinewy left arm in a sweep that took in Jackson's Creek and the sprawling land to the west as it swept across a wide slice of Kansas.

Cramer nodded. 'You find that out for yourself, or did somebody come along, point the way?' He pointed to his own eyes, then at the brave, then beyond to where the brave had indicated. The brave frowned, looked at La Roche, but again Cramer jumped in.

'Farrall. The man with the badge.' He pointed to the front of his bloodstained shirt, drew a crude star. 'He told you where to go, ain't that right? Promised you a heap of whiskey if you'd snatch the kid?' And to make it clear, he placed his hand alongside his mouth and flapped it open and closed like a man doing some loose talking.

And now the big brave grinned. He nodded, said emphatically, 'Farr . . . all!'

and the word was picked up by one of the other braves who, like Cramer, lifted his hand to his mouth. But he held his fist clenched, as if holding a bottle, and he let his head fall back and tilted the imaginary bottle, then kicked his pony into a trot and guided it in a staggering circle while he swayed drunkenly on its back.

The other braves rocked with laughter, nodding furiously, the name Farrall bouncing back and forth. Watching them, Cramer reached down, slid the Winchester out of its boot, swiftly jacked a shell into the breech and blasted a shot at the clear blue skies.

The laughter stopped, as if cut by a knife. The big Indian didn't even blink. Cramer allowed himself a tight smile, then tossed the rifle to the brave. He caught it, swung the pony away, and was at once surrounded by the other four braves who moved in to admire and touch the gleaming weapon.

'Satisfied?' La Roche's face was puzzled.

'Passable.'

'You care to tell me what you were talkin' about?'

'When we've got water between us and them,' Cramer said. 'Won't be too long before that buck starts lookin' for live targets.'

'Ain't that a fact!' La Roche breathed, and without more ado he spurred his horse into a dead run for the river.

Joel Cramer took one last, hungry look at the Indian village. The white boy had been released by the squaw and was trotting unsteadily across the dusty, uneven ground towards a cluster of naked children splashing in a muddy pool. He was chubby and fair-haired, but his eyes were as blue as the endless skies.

Emotionlessly, his face wooden, Cramer turned away and rode hard after Jak La Roche.

12

'Sure,' Jak La Roche said, 'I've heard of Padraig Flynn and that ranch of his, Blue Stack.'

It was late afternoon, shadows lengthening, the weary horses hobbled and grazing. They had ridden a hard three miles, keen to put distance between them and the Comanche brave with his gleaming new Winchester, then another three before they'd stopped to rest the horses and slake their thirst at the same creek they'd crossed twice in little more than twelve hours. After that, more miles, across stretches of naked hard-pan where the dust rose in choking clouds, across endless prairie where the horses whispered through hockhigh, cooling grass, always with the ribbon of water to their right, always with stands of cottonwoods along the banks of the creek when they needed shade; always, too, with the disquieting conviction that if they were, now, heading in the direction that would take them to the heartless man responsible for the kidnapping of Cramer's boy, somewhere along the way there would be a bunch of armed men waiting in ambush, with orders to turn them back or shoot them down like dogs.

Several times they picked up the trail laid by the wounded lawman, Butch Farrall. Each time, Cramer looked at Jak La Roche, tightened his lips and pushed onwards.

Now, in the cooling shade of the cottonwoods where he had been forced to call a halt before the wrung-out horses suffered permanent damage — and where, if the truth be known, he needed time to gather his thoughts — Joel Cramer trickled smoke and looked across at the Louisiana gambler sitting cross-legged against the bole of a tree.

'I've been lookin' for the man behind a kidnap. If you knew about Blue Stack, why keep it to yourself?'

'You were fixated, Tucson. Dyke Manson was your man. Nothing I could have said would've changed that.' La Roche absently polished the battered harmonica on the sleeve of his check jacket, then added pointedly, 'Besides which, me bein' a stranger in these parts you know damn near as much as me about Flynn, and his Blue Stack spread.'

'Yeah. I guess I heard the name a couple of times, let it slide by when I should have pressed the point.'

'Maybe. But when a kid's been snatched, a woman murdered,' La Roche said, 'the last place you go lookin' is the ranch owned by an honest man.'

'But now we do,' Cramer said, 'because after that Indian all the signs are pointin' his way.'

La Roche reflected on that, then raised the harmonica to his lips, closed his eyes, blew a series of plaintive, reedy notes then segued flawlessly into the

'Battle Hymn of the Republic'. Cramer settled back and rested his head against his saddle, eyes narrowed to slits, letting the familar tune work its magic as it washed over him, soothing frayed nerves while at the same time bringing the prickle of tears to eyes raw from the dust of the trail.

'We've got talking to do,' he said at last, drawing a shaky breath and flicking away his cigarette as the music trailed into silence and sadness felt for battles won and loved ones lost became a pointless indulgence. 'What we've got ahead of us would strain the relationship of close pards — and I don't see us like that, just yet.'

'Oh, we're closer than you could possibly imagine,' La Roche said. There was a slight tremor in his voice. He knocked spittle out of the harmonica, again rubbed the bright metal on his sleeve. When he looked up, his eyes were luminous in the evening light.

'I told you,' Cramer said quietly. 'Feller I killed down in Laredo, his name wasn't Pierre. Far as I could tell before the lights started goin' out in that *cantina*, it was Luke, or some such.'

'Close,' La Roche said, 'but you misheard. They called him Lucky, and that was ironic because when he was dealing poker the last person Pierre relied on was that painted lady.'

'Who was the first?' Cramer said. 'Or is that me bein' stupid?'

La Roche breathed softly on the harmonica, wiped away the mist of condensation and was still staring intently at his hands as he said, 'I was the only one, because who else is going to rub shoulders with a man who murdered his crippled pa for no damn reason except he needed cash in a hurry?'

'Sweet Jesus!' Cramer said softly. 'And you stuck by him, rode with him clear across Texas — then blame me for his death?'

But La Roche hadn't heard, or didn't want to.

'Ma had been dead ten years, taken by the fever. Pierre rode in swayin' and cursin' and stinkin' of whiskey after a night on the town, shot Pa in the back when he was gettin' supper off the stove, whacked me over the head when I flew at him. I came to, belly down over my horse, bleedin' like a stuck pig, ten miles from our home in Lafayette with Pierre settin' those horses at a dead run for the Sabine River and Texas.'

The memories seemed too much for La Roche. He bent to blow fiercely into the harmonica, set it wailing high and long in a snatch of mournful tunefulness that set the hairs on Joel Cramer's neck prickling, snatched it away to look brighteyed at Cramer. He said, 'For two years I handed over my honest winnings to make up for the dollars he scraped together by cheatin', and all the time . . . ' He stopped, swallowed hard. 'And all the time I was sleepin' and eatin' and playin' cards in smoky *cantinas* and waitin' for the right moment . . . lookin' for something inside me that would tell me, now, right now, take the lousy, murderin' bastard . . . my brother . . . '

The silence was so tight it crackled. An errant breeze ruffled the cottonwoods. Cramer felt the stiffness in his shoulders, his back. He said softly, 'Instead, a feller called Tucson showed up, did the job you couldn't stomach.'

La Roche sighed raggedly. 'How do you go about thankin' a man for killing your brother? We came together in a blaze of guns, put paid to them goddamn *Rurales* then parted in the rain . . . '

'So when we met again, by chance, after fifteen years, you hung on,' Cramer nodded. 'Of course. I saw hate in your eyes, last night in the woods, and thought it was for me. But that was just memories causing pain while you did the same as you did all those years ago with your brother . . . waited for the right moment.'

'And now we're ridin' into something,' La Roche said, 'would strain the friendship of close pards.' And he looked up and dispelled the aura of gloom hanging over the cottonwoods with a grin as pure and bright as sun-struck water. 'So, as one pard to another, tell me how you read this.'

'That,' Cramer said, matching the little gambler's coruscating grin, 'is a mite more difficult.'

He dug out the makings and began fashioning a cigarette, letting the familiar routine jostle his thoughts into some sort of order while La Roche exchanged the battered harmonica for an equally battered tin canteen and with lukewarm water washed the taste of bitter memories from his mouth, spat them onto the grass.

A blue haze of smoke drifted about Cramer's head. Insects hummed lazily in the dying heat of day. In the near distance, to the east, Jackson's Creek was the lazy lapping of water on stones, the sudden splash of a leaping fish.

He watched La Roche wander across to his horse in the warm evening sunshine, talk softly to it, run his pale gambler's hands across the slick, flattened hair where the saddle had weighed heavy on the thick blanket. And he thought about the separate trails he and the Louisiana gambler had ridden from Laredo, trails that had taken them different ways around a savage land only for them to wind up in the same damn place, at the same damn time. Maybe La Roche was right; maybe they were closer than he could possibly imagine, drawn together in a chance meeting that began and ended in violence. But with La Roche's explanation, the matter of their association was either dead and buried, or set to lead somewhere ... and that quandary was something to mull over at another, more favourable time. For now, there were questions to be answered and, as La Roche walked back across the springy grass and his boots rustled through the crisp dead leaves lying in the dappled shade under the cottonwoods, Cramer began to use words to feel his way towards the truth.

'You've seen what I've seen, listened to that Comanche brave. That wasn't a lie conjured up so's he could claim a shiny new rifle. I've got to take it he was tellin' the truth. But if Padraig Flynn is an honest cattleman, why would he arrange a child's kidnap, the murder of a woman, Jak?'

'And pay for the dirty work with a heap of gold eagles?' La Roche pursed his lips. 'If it was Dyke Manson, he'd have reasons that'd chill a man's soul. If it was Padraig Flynn . . . '

'Maybe I'm talkin' because I already know the answer,' Cramer said. 'Like, one man's loss is another man's gain.'

'Or woman's,' La Roche suggested, tossing the canteen to Cramer. 'Remember that squaw?'

'Sure. So the wife of Padraig Flynn sees her child taken by Comanche, grieves so bad her man waits just long enough so the kid's appearance — any kid — ain't going to matter, then talks to men like Wood, Lawson — maybe goin' through Manson and Farrell to get to them — and sets them lookin' for a replacement?'

'Yeah. And, glory be, in rides a poor sodbuster and his wife to set up home on Manson's land, bringin' with them a tow-headed kid just about the right age.'

'That's right. The Flynn woman's boy was taken from the crib at four weeks, gets returned nine months later. The kid she gets back is tow-headed like he should be, twenty pounds heavier which is also what she'd expect. So, who's to know?'

Cramer drank from the water bottle, tossed it back to La Roche and thought about the boy in the Indian village, the son who'd been snatched from his wife's embrace.

'But she'd know, wouldn't she, this Flynn woman, if her boy's eyes had changed colour.'

La Roche shrugged. 'You're talkin' to

the wrong man. I ain't never been hitched. But it seems to me, if a woman grieves for a child long enough, then gets one seems like it might be hers placed all soft and helpless in her arms — well, wouldn't it be natural for her to look into those innocent eyes and start convincin' herself her memory's playin' tricks, they'd been blue all along?'

'Brown,' Cramer said, remembering.

'You see,' La Roche said, smiling.

'But why kill?'

'Hired hands,' La Roche said. 'That wasn't part of the deal, but when it happened Flynn was in too deep to renege on payment, or refuse to take the child — more so if his wife was already holdin' him tight to her breast.'

Cramer nodded pensively.

'You wondered what I was gettin' at, those questions I was throwin at that brave back there at the Indian village?'

'I got the gist. You're thinkin' Farrall arranged for Flynn's kid to be snatched, paid the Indians with moonshine from Manson's still. But why would he do that? What the hell would he gain?'

'Nothing,' Cramer said softly, 'at the time. But I mentioned Farrall's deviousness once before. What if he arranged the snatch, knowing damn well he could take the kid back from the Indians when they'd drunk all that moonshine and were runnin' up a thirst. He did that, he'd get paid by Flynn, and his reputation'd be sky high.'

'Goddamn!' La Roche shook his head. 'Then you came along, and he saw a way of raisin' his stock with Flynn and still keepin' on the right side of the Comanche.'

'It explains a lot. Like, why he was intent on runnin' me out of town, why he came after us with that Crow tracker, Ike Goldfink. He'd figured he was dealin' with a sodbuster used to workin' a plough. But he saw my name on a wanted dodger, realized the men doin' his dirty work had snatched Tucson Joel Cramer's kid, murdered his wife. Hell, all of a sudden he was all tangled up with a gunslinger. He knew damn well I'd dig deep to get at the killers, then go after him. Even if I took a fatal slug, chances were the story'd come out — and if his part in the original snatch reached Flynn, he'd be finished.'

Cramer smoked on in silence while La Roche stowed the canteen, found a hunk of jerky in his saddle-bags and sat down against the bole of his tree to gnaw at the dry meat. The skies were darkening to the east, the only sounds were those of the river, and the browsing horses, yet more than once Cramer found his eyes drifting towards the west where lay the Blue Stack ranch, his ears pricked for the sound of approaching horsemen but his thoughts ranging far ahead.

He should have been elated. Instead, he was jumpy, his feelings all wrong. Hell, the pressing questions had been answered — or most of the answers worked out — and all that was left was for him to push on to Padraig Flynn's spread and take what was his by right. There would be armed opposition, because Padraig Flynn had chosen to step outside the law and for him there could be no going back. But violence was no stranger to the man who rode under the name of Tucson, and as Cramer trickled smoke and watched the Louisiana gambler exercising his jaws on a hunk of meat as tough as old leather, he knew that the cause of his disquiet lay deeper; his own innate decency had become a stumbling block.

'If I take the boy now,' he said into the clean, cooling air, 'I'm no better than Padraig Flynn.' He shook his head, felt the hard ache in his throat, sensed that La Roche had stopped chewing to listen and said, 'I thought I'd found my boy, Jak, but he's as far away from me now as he ever was.'

13

They saddled up and rode away from the cotton-woods when the far western sky was a wide strip of brilliant gold-splashed crimson spanning the horizon, the thin mists that had dissipated during the heat of the day now gathering again in cold hollows and on the deep-shadowed flanks of silent woods to chill them to the bone as they rode with haste towards Padraig Flynn's Blue Stack.

Before leaving Jackson's Creek they had washed down the remains of La Roche's jerky, refilled their canteens and taken a few minutes to assess their weaponry. Deprived of the Winchester he had handed to the Indian brave in the confrontation outside their village, Cramer knew he would be forced to rely on the six-gun pouched in a gunbelt whose loops were filled with gleaming cartridges — which meant in anything other than a close range, stand-up-and-knock-'em-down fight, he would be worse than useless. Jak La Roche had the Colt he habitually kept tucked in his belt, and a couple of cartons of shells that would be shared between the pistol and his '73 Winchester, but all the weapons in the West, Cramer thought ruefully, wouldn't turn a gambler into a gunslinger.

'Only thing we can do,' La Roche said, poker-faced, when Cramer voiced his thoughts, 'is creep up behind them and shoot 'em in the back.'

Spoken in jest, maybe — but Cramer knew the little gambler's estimation of the chances was too damn close to the truth for comfort.

As they pressed on away from the river the gently sloping wooded terrain levelled out to give way to a fissured landscape of low hills cut by deep arroyos and dry washes. Trees became sparse. Without their cover the rising winds of the approaching night drove away the hanging mists but replaced their chill with a cold that cut like a sharp knife.

Huddled miserably in his jacket, hunched in the saddle and peering about him with eyes narrowed against the biting wind, it seemed to Cramer that the darkening land through which they were riding was uncannily similar to the serrated country beyond the shallow ford where Goldfink and Farrall had been bested. In an effort to lift his gloomy mood he vowed to look on that similarity as an omen of good, figuring that what they had achieved once, they could easily do again. At once, his spirits rose: the law of averages was still with him, the man who went on the attack when by rights he should be dead would come out top of the heap. He grinned savagely. They would overcome the armed men driving their horses hard down the trail from Blue Stack, or already lurking in ambush. And after that . . . Cramer shook his head in the gathering darkness, not daring to voice his optimism, the grin transformed into an ugly grimace as he tightened his jaw.

The cold winds hissed across the short grass. Behind them, clouds rolled in from the east, bringing the first spatters of rain. The drops were ice-cold on his neck, but there could be nothing as cold as the thought of a life stretching ahead of him without the boy who was his life. So, first deal with the men Padraig Flynn had certainly dispatched to turn him back. And after that —

'Riders to both sides, Tucson — been there for some ways.'

'I've been daydreaming,' Cramer said, inwardly cursing. 'You mean they've been ridin' with us, but makin' no move.'

'Shadows, out on both flanks, keepin' their distance — and I can see only one reason why they'd do that.'

Cramer grunted. 'We're ridin' into a trap.'

'Right. They're cattlemen turned

sheepherder, makin' damn sure a couple of stupid sheep don't take a wrong turn.'

'Then we won't,' Cramer said. 'Forewarned is forearmed — ain't that the saying?'

'I can think up one or two of my own,' La Roche said caustically, 'but not one of 'em'd stop a bullet.'

They rode on, clattering down a slope and across a dry creek bed from where the hard beat of horses' hooves rose, and was deadened, by the darkness of the night. They emerged with trepidation into a murky landscape lit eerily by the rising moon, where pale shadows raced across the undulating grassland as rain-clouds scudded across the moon's face. No more than 400 yards ahead, a long, dark ridge formed a natural barrier. It stretched as far south as Cramer could see, but ended abruptly in a high bluff a mile or so to the north. The trail ahead was a narrow strip of rutted earth, following the contours of the land as it cut across the prairie as if aiming for a deep notch cut into the centre of the ridge and its blanket of trees.

There was no sign of their sinister escort.

'Done with shepherding,' Cramer surmised as they eased back, slowed their horses to a walk. 'P Bar F's got to be over yonder, on the other side of that ridge. The land this side ain't cattle country; this trail ain't much used. My guess is Jackson's Creek loops to the west beyond that bluff, givin' Flynn all the water he needs and allows him to feed his cows on lush grass. But that notch in the ridge is the way we're bein' forced to go . . . ' — he pointed along the trail — 'and up there's where they'll make their move.'

La Roche was only half listening, bridle metal jingling as he twisted in his saddle in an attempt to scan a 360° horizon without falling off his horse. He turned one way, grabbed the horn as his horse stood in a rut, twisted for a final glance down the back-trail then turned his face to the trail ahead. The wind gusted, lifting the brim of his Stetson. His rain-spattered countenance glistened in the moonlight.

Watching him, Cramer grinned. He said quietly, 'My earlier offer stands, Jak. This is my fight, still as good a time as any for you to cut and run. If I did you and the world a favour takin' Pierre out of circulation, you've more than paid your dues.'

'Cuttin' and runnin' might be a good idea for both of us,' La Roche said grimly, 'seein' as three hombres who maybe figure we ain't seen them have just rode out of that timber high up on that ridge, and their partners have closed up behind.'

'It seems like I'm blind to what's goin' on,' Cramer said disgustedly, 'even when my mind's on the job.' As he spoke, the thud of hooves reached his ears, carried on another sharp gust of wind that lifted the horses' tails. Up on the ridge, the three horsemen who had carelessly emerged from the trees had now pulled back into the shadows, their position revealed by the fitful moonlight glinting on their weapons, the sheen of their horses.

'I can't take them with a pistol,' Cramer said. 'With the Winchester, you'd get maybe one or two.'

'Don't bet on it!'

With a swift glance back down the trail, Cramer said, 'How many riders were doin' the shepherding?'

'It was gettin' dark, fleeting glimpses is all I got. If I was forced to make a guess — no more than two or three.'

'There's two behind us, riding stirrup, holding back. They're leaving the shooting to their pards up ahead. Last time we saw Farrall he was plugged in the shoulder and losing a lot of blood. But he's built like an ox, and he was heading in this direction. There ain't nobody else could've warned Flynn, so I expect Farrall to be with the Blue Stack hands up there on the ridge. Maybe he'll do some talkin', point out the error of our ways — though from my limited experience of that miserable excuse for a town marshal, I doubt that. Either way, we've got maybe a couple of minutes to play it their way, or make some sort of a move.'

La Roche pursed his lips, looked about him, spat into the wind. 'If you reckon Blue Stack land is beyond that bluff,' he said slowly, 'could be the long way round's our only chance.'

Swiftly, Cramer calculated the line they'd need to take to reach the bluff in the shortest possible time, felt the first stirring of hope as he saw a clear path across open grassland with nothing barring their way but the occasional hillock or isolated stand of trees.

His hopes rose higher when he turned to look critically at the ridge. The pines thickly blanketing its upper slopes dipped down at one point in a long spur that curled to the south and reached almost to the level plain and the end of the trail. Before they could hope to cut off Cramer and La Roche, the three riders waiting on the ridge would need to ride down the steep slope — forced by the nature of the terrain to head in the wrong direction — then round that spur of trees. That delay, Cramer estimated, could mean the difference between their gettin' to the bluff, or gettin' shot.

'The trail ain't exactly level, or straight,' La Roche said, watching Cramer. 'We ride on a couple of hundred yards we're gonna catch 'em by surprise when we do take off. Just about there we hit the easy grade that marks the lower slopes of that ridge. The trail narrows, trees get thicker to either side, the only way to go is through a dry winter run-off lies ahead. What I can see, it wriggles to the north for a spell. When it finally peters out, it'll have taken us maybe fifty yards closer to where we want to go.'

'And deep enough so those fellers behind'll lose sight of us.' Cramer breathed tightly, squinting through the gloom at the dry wash La Roche had spotted. 'When we do come out of that

191

draw we'll be on the west side of a low hillock. Those fellers up on the ridge'll have us in their sights most of the way, but by the time those behind pick us up again we'll have gained a hundred yards.'

Spurs chinked. The horses' gait picked up to a stretched-out lope. A glance behind showed the two riders still holding back, riding stirrup and showing no concern at the change of pace. Nor should they, Cramer thought grimly. As far as they were concerned, the faster he and La Roche rode, the sooner they'd be heading up the slope into the waiting guns of their pards on the ridge.

Then the trail in front of them sloped and they were clattering up into the dry wash. As La Roche had surmised, the run-off that carried away the winter floodwater cut into the almost flat, lower slopes of the ridge, then took a loop to the north. Once in the gully, Cramer urged his horse into a fast gallop, riding recklessly over rutted, stony ground. The thin moonlight was chopped off by the high walls of washed-out rock, creating pools of inky shadow through which the two men rode blind. Just once Cramer risked a snatched glance up at the gully's jagged rim to his left and saw, with an immense surge of exhilaration, that the tall pines at the lower point of the drooping spur had cut them off from the watchers high on the ridge. And he laughed out loud at the thought of the gunmen ahead and to the rear, straining their eyes to follow the thin cloud of dust that rose into the moonlight from the dry wash to be torn apart by the wind.

His laughter was echoed by La Roche, riding hard, nose to tail, their harsh guffaws slapping back off the stone walls to be swallowed by the clatter of hooves then picked up and carried high and wide by the gusting wind that moaned icily through the draw.

And then, without warning, they

were out and clear.

Close behind him, La Roche yelled excitedly, 'Go, Tucson, ride like the wind!'

The trail split, the left fork curving sharply to skirt the wooded spur then take a zig-zag climb to the top of the ridge. In too short a time, that was the way the gunmen on the ridge would come riding hell for leather, larruping their horses in fury as they realized they had been fooled. So it was the right fork that Cramer took, spurring hard then stretching low along his horse's flowing mane as he pushed it along in the lee of the grassy ridge that hid them from their armed, unwanted escort out on the plain. His eyes were fixed on the distant bluff, outlined against the wind-torn night skies. His back crawled, waiting for the bite of hot lead.

The first shot came as the grassy hillock fell away to their right and they emerged from its shelter into a fierce wind sweeping needles of driving rain across the open prairie. But the shot came from on high, the riders' first knowledge of it the solid thump and the heavy clod of wet dirt gouged out of the trail ahead. Then came the flat crack of the rifle, the eddying sound instantly whipped away. Another slug whirred across Cramer's shoulder, a third plucked at his sleeve. And now, from out on the prairie there came the distant sound of raised voices. Then nothing. A silence. And the sudden, insistent drumming of hooves.

'They've put their rifles away, their mind to riding!' La Roche cried, coming alongside Cramer's horse as around them the ground flattened, leaving them exposed. 'The chase is on, feller!'

They rode abreast, racing a fast-moving shadow that rippled over grassland and the flat rock and stunted mesquite lining the trail as clouds scudded across the moon. Outpaced by nature's sheer power and speed, they were overtaken and enveloped in darkness, buffeted by the wind, relying on the instinct and sure-footedness of their mounts to carry them through clumped chaparral and over treacherously uneven ground fast enough to keep ahead of the two men who would be streaking across the prairie to cut them off.

The moon came and went, floating between low, streaming clouds, directing its shafts of light here and there at random like a giant, swinging lantern. In one such shifting pool of brilliance Cramer caught a glimpse of the two men who had been behind them at the draw. Far out on the flank, they were ghostly mounted figures streaking through a sweeping curtain of rain, keeping pace but riding a parallel course without closing.

Why? They were closer than the men on the ridge, but making no move. At best, Cramer would have expected a volley of shots intended to bring down their horses; at worst a direct assault with blazing pistols aimed at the slaughter of men and beasts.

Then, overhead, ripped asunder by the storm, the skies cleared. The wind's moan subsided to an aching sigh; the rain died away and lambent moonlight flooded the land. And suddenly, as they drew near to the bluff, the rumble of pounding hooves rolled like thunder from behind them.

'Two of 'em!' La Roche yelled, glancing over his shoulder. 'The one on the big grey'll be Hawker. But there was three on the ridge, so why two, Tucson?'

His answer came swiftly, and with a deadly impact that caused Cramer to bare his teeth in savage frustration. Where the trail cut past a jumble of massive fallen boulders on the ridge's lower slopes before rounding the vertical fall of the high bluff, a horseman appeared. He plunged recklessly down from the ridge through rough scrub, a gross man of enormous bulk whose upper body was clothed in black and whose hair was a thick black plait streaming in the wind. As the distance between them closed, Cramer could clearly see, through eyes narrowed with despair, the naked blade of the big knife tucked in this man's leather waist-belt.

Then what had been an extraordinary riding feat became an act of impossible bravado and unbelievable gun prowess. Urged on by its rider, Dyke Manson's black horse took the last twenty feet of the slope in a high-flying bound that carried it like a bird onto the trail. And while it was stretching out in that prodigious leap of spine-tingling grace, the shotgun held by the stock in Manson's meaty right hand belched flame.

Jak La Roche's horse went down in a tangle of legs and thick clods of flying earth. A sharp crack told sickeningly that one of those legs had snapped. The little gambler hit the wet trail in a tight ball and rolled. He tumbled into the tight-knit chaparral with a roar of anger and pain, climbed to his feet with thorns ripping his clothes and flesh and went for his six-gun.

Cramer dragged his horse to a halt so sudden it sat back on its haunches, came up again in a fearsome lunge that snapped him back in the saddle. That violent jerk spoiled his draw. Fighting to stay on the horse, he grabbed one-handed for the horn, with the other fumbled for his .45. But he was a mile out, his clawed fingers finding only slick leather as the horse dropped a foreleg in a hole and toppled sideways with a shrill whinny.

The fall saved Cramer's life. With all the skill of his still-living forebears, Dyke Manson sat easily atop his dancing mount and swung the shot-gun. The muzzle unerringly fixed on Cramer's struggling horse, spewed flame and smoke and a deadly hail of scattered lead.

But Cramer was down, flinging himself sideways — too late — as the horse crashed heavily down on his leg. He heard the rain of buckshot tear into the saddle, cringed to the horse's agonized squeal as hot lead tore its neck. He heard the sharp crack of a six-gun, knew that La Roche had entered the fray. But over that sound he heard the rapidly swelling beat of approaching hooves. His own horse was kicking and snorting. La Roche's mount was a lifeless hulk, lying in a pool of blood. Cramer took an agonized glance back down the trail and saw the two riders bearing down on the bloody tangle of downed men and horses.

About to be surrounded by five gunmen, with one leg trapped under his kicking horse, Tucson Joel Cramer drew his six-gun, cocked it, and prepared to fight to the death.

14

Cramer's horse snorted in fear. The air reeked of burnt gunpowder. With a fierce yell, Jak La Roche tore himself from the chaparral's thorny embrace and leaped alongside the trapped gunslinger. As he stood over Cramer in a protective crouch and began snapping shots at the dark bulk of Dyke Manson, the downed horse kicked mightily, found purchase with its hind legs and lurched to its feet.

From being pinned down and helpless beneath a warm mound of struggling horse-flesh, suddenly Cramer was free. He rolled, cursed softly as the wounded horse's frantic exertions splashed him with hot blood, then gritted his teeth and groaned as pain lanced through his leg. He collided heavily with La Roche, heard him roar in anger then realized that his fury, too, was directed at the horse, which had tossed its head in panic, slammed against his shoulder and ruined his aim.

'Get to Hell and gone, you devil!'

With a mighty slap, La Roche sent Cramer's mount galloping down the trail, mane flying, stirrups flapping. Crazed with fear, it headed straight for Dyke Manson. The 'breed was broadside, blocking the trail, controlling his frisky mount with his massive thighs as he rammed shells into the scattergun.

Then hooves thundered, bearing rapidly down on Cramer and La Roche, and both men turned to face the new danger.

Cramer was on his feet, favouring his bad leg, awkwardly braced. He cast a swift glance towards Manson, saw his black horse stagger then prance sideways on stiff legs as Cramer's mount barged past and the big 'breed was forced to forget about reloading and put all his effort into staying in the saddle.

When he looked back along the trail

the two men who had ridden the long way down from the ridge were closing fast.

'We're too exposed here!' La Roche cried.

'Only cover around,' Cramer snapped, 'is that heap of rocks,' then loosed two rapid shots at the approaching riders.

'All right, if that's our only chance,' La Roche said, and immediately set off like a jack-rabbit across the trail, making for the massive rock fall. He was halfway there when Manson let loose with the first barrel of the scattergun. La Roche's feet were cut from under him. Dirt spouted. He went down, seemed to bounce off the packed earth, took off in a flying leap for the safety of the rocks — and the two riders bearing down on them opened up with a withering hail of hot lead.

Bullets sang off the rocks, lending their eerie song to the mournful whining of the wind. But La Roche was down and safe, wriggling behind the biggest boulder as needle-sharp rock splinters keened into the night. He screamed, 'Move yourself, Tucson!' and risked his neck to blast a shot that caused one of the approaching horsemen to veer sharply.

But, jaw clenched, caught in the open, Cramer knew he was in bad trouble. He took a raking stride towards the rocks, but staggered and almost went down as his leg buckled. Manson's triumphant laugh was the ghastly howl of a hunting wolf. The shotgun's second barrel blazed, the flame dimming the moon, its roar deafening. The scattered shot ripped through Cramer's shirt as he flung himself aside and twisted his torso. He felt his back slashed by a thousand red-hot knife blades. Pain lanced through his body, gripped him by the throat, choked off his breath.

Gasping, unbalanced, he reeled towards the cover of the rocks, the two gunmen now close enough for him to see, in a horrifying blur, the glaring whites of their horses' eyes, the warm wet mist of their breath snorted into the cold night air from flared nostrils. A pistol cracked, spat flame. The bullet sang wide. Cramer was dimly aware of a silence behind him as Dyke Manson again snatched precious seconds to reload. Then the two riders were upon him, riding on with their pace unslackened. The man determined to ride Cramer down was Marshal Butch Farrall. As he hurtled out of the night, a savage grin split his dark, greasy countenance. The ragged stub of a cigar was clenched between yellow teeth. He drew alongside, leaned out of the saddle. His arm lifted, swung down viciously as he used his pistol like a club. The gleaming .45's barrel missed Cramer's skull but grazed his cheek and slammed against his collar bone. His arm went dead. His pistol fell from nerveless fingers.

Almost dragged out of the saddle by weakness and the ferocity of the blow, Farrall sawed on the reins and pulled his horse around in a tight turn that brought it squealing to its knees. As he spun, teeth bared with strain, his booted foot came up out of the stirrup and slammed stiff-legged into Cramer's chest. The piston-like blow drove him backwards. Spurs chinked musically as his heels hit rock, and now, at last, he began to go down. Strength flowed out of him like water. His eyes rolled. High above him the moon's disc spun sickeningly in a shifting sea of light and shade. He seemed to float, waiting an eternity for his tormented body to slam into hard rock . . .

★ ★ ★

'You're OK.' Jak La Roche's voice floated to him through the mist, 'except that shirt of yours has seen better days.'

A smooth palm slapped his face, came back and hard knuckles cracked against his cheekbone. He blinked, shook his head, felt the stickiness of wet blood pooling around his waist and said hoarsely, 'How long?'

'A matter of seconds.' Then, the tone insistent, the message like a knife-blade piercing Cramer's befuddled brain, 'Snap out of it, Tucson, remember your boy — '

The Louisiana gambler broke off, snapped a shot over the big rock, slid down with his back against stone and thumbed shells into the cylinder. Again the shotgun blasted, and it became clear to Cramer as his senses sluggishly returned that Dyke Manson was down off his black horse and working his way on foot along the steep lower slopes. The scatter-gun's powerful blast had sent lead shot screaming from the boulders on their right side. If he makes it any further, Cramer thought, we'll both of us take the next barrel in the back.

'What about Hawker?'

'Funny thing,' La Roche said, 'but that Pueblo gunslinger took off across the grass towards them two been escortin' us from a safe distance. Then I heard shootin' — '

Cramer's arm slammed across, knocking him flat.

Like an immense black bear, Butch Farrall seemed to rise out of the earth as he clambered up on top of the rock fall, loose shirt stiff with blood and flapping in the wind. His hair was wild, his thick legs spread and braced, his eyes wide and staring in the moonlight. The pistol in his meaty fist was already swinging to bear on Cramer. With La Roche wriggling like a beached fish under him, Cramer fumbled for his six-gun, felt the prickle of fear as he found an empty holster, turned desperately to La Roche. But, looming like a thick oak tree above him, Butch Farrall was already throwing down, the .45's hammer socking back with an audible snap.

'Gotcha, you bastard!' he roared.

Muzzle flame flared orange. But in the instant that it took for the hammer to fall on the cap and the powder to explode, there was a roar to match the beefy marshal's bellow and the crack of his pistol then turn both into a whisper that was lost beneath a tremendous eruption of sound and dazzling light.

Butch Farrall was blown backwards, lifted bodily off the rock-fall. He fell with arms and legs outstretched and bulging eyes already glazed; above his belt-buckle a ragged, gaping hole in his belly that glinted a slick red in the light of the moon.

Stray lead shot whined off the rock, hissed through the grass. In the awful silence, it was as if Dyke Manson was stunned. He was ten yards up the slope, the discharged shotgun that had killed the marshal of Jackson's Bend limp in his grasp. The black, button eyes were looking blindly beyond the rock-fall.

Heaving Joel Cramer off him with all the strength in his slight frame, the Louisiana gambler shot Dyke Manson between those eyes as he came out of shock, hissed like a snake and went for his knife. Even then it was touch and go. The 'breed's big hand was a blur as it snapped to his belt and came up to flip the broad-bladed knife in a back-hand throw. But he was already dead. Dyke Manson went down soundlessly. The point of the knife drew sparks from the rock behind La Roche, the shotgun fell with the hollow clatter of empty metal.

* * *

'None of this was Padraig Flynn's idea.'

The stocky man with the sharp blue eyes was shamefaced, pointedly keeping his gaze averted from the body of Abe Hawker tied belly down over his own grey gelding.

'All right,' Joel Cramer said, his voice tight from cold and the strain of keeping his breathing shallow, 'tell me what was his idea.'

'I'm foreman of Blue Stack,' the man said. 'Frank Cooper. I don't know the rights or wrongs of what's goin' on, but

Flynn's idea was for you and him to talk.'

'He calls this talk!' said Jak La Roche.

'We set out to put that to you,' Cooper said doggedly to Cramer. He shrugged. 'Farrall and Manson had other ideas . . . them, and that feller Hawker.'

'We downed him when he tried to suck us in, got sore when we refused.' This was the second man, a lean character with a dragoon moustache, patiently sitting his horse outside the circle. 'You could at least thank us for that.'

'All that tells me is you can use those pistols you've got hangin' from your belts.'

The lean man laughed. 'There's two more at Blue Stack can draw faster, shoot straighter. As you'll find out, if the talkin' don't go Flynn's way.'

'Assuming we go there,' Cramer said.

Frank Cooper shifted in the saddle, looked at Cramer's hunched, bloody form atop his horse, the slight figure of the Louisiana gambler. He sighed, shook his head and spat to one side.

'You'll go,' he said. 'One way or another.'

15

The ride across the prairie to Blue
Stack was through blustering wind and
intermittent rain that chilled the body
and planted the seeds of despair in the
soul. It tore at the pathetic dregs of Joel
Cramer's strength and left him ragged
and wrung-out, a strong man who
swayed in the saddle of his bleeding
horse like a bowed reed as the quartet
of horsemen — leading a grey horse
bearing a dead man who dripped a trail
of blood — rode under the rough
timber crossbar and onto the domain of
Padraig Flynn.

Through bleary eyes Cramer saw
a house ablaze with lamplight that
flooded the yard from wide windows, a
sturdy corral where the ranch's working
cavvy dozed with their tails to the wind,
barns and outhouses set back against
tall trees, a backdrop of low hills

drenched in cold moonlight.

In front of the house, a man stood straight and tall, his dark frock coat tight across wide shoulders, pants tucked into polished boots. And as he looked at that man, then lifted his gaze to those windows from which lamplight flooded, Joel Cramer's laboured breathing caught in his throat and eyes that were dim with weariness suddenly became clear.

In one of those windows, standing sideways at the drapes with her head turned to gaze out, a woman with blonde hair arched her back gracefully as she held a tow-headed boy at her hip.

An inarticulate sound tumbled from Cramer's lips. He touched his horse with spurs that chinked musically, started it away from the other men and across the yard. If he had made it that far, he would have ridden over the tall man without noticing; taken the horse up the wide timber steps and on into the house . . .

'Far enough!' Padraig Flynn said clearly.

And only then did Cramer notice that, once again, he was up against a man whose chosen weapon was the shotgun, and that shotgun was levelled at his chest.

'You've got my boy,' he said. 'Only time it'll be far enough is when I'm standin' next to him.'

'Back off. Turn around, ride into the barn.'

Padraig Flynn's eyes were the blue of tempered steel. He let his words sink in, held the shotgun steady while Cramer did some thinking.

'I'm gettin' kinda sick of men with Greeners loaded with buckshot,' Cramer said. He was aware of his own dead weight in the saddle, of the ponderous weight of his six-gun against his thigh. Knew that, in the past — perhaps even now, if he could summon his full strength — he would have drawn and fired before the elegant man confronting him could squeeze the trigger. Frank Cooper and the lean man with the dragoon moustache had melted away, taking the grey horse and its gruesome burden with them as they moved out of the pool of lamplight. A taut silence had settled uneasily over the yard. Cramer's eyes lifted. In the wide window the woman with the tow-headed boy drifted away in the room's warm glow, and was gone.

Pain knifed through Cramer's heart. Without thought, his right hand lifted, moved away from his body —

'Tucson!'

Jak La Roche spoke softly. Cramer blinked. Padraig Flynn shrugged, wagged the shotgun muzzle from side to side in a clear warning.

'We need to talk.'

'I could take you,' Cramer said dispassionately.

'But not them, too.'

And behind Cramer there was the metallic sound of weapons cocking, and he knew that in this yard at Blue Stack there was more than one shotgun.

216

La Roche made the decision. He turned his horse and walked it away to skirt the corral and ride straignt through the gaping doors of the big barn and vanish into the gloom. Cramer took a breath, then dragged his eyes away from the house to wheel his mount and follow the little gambler.

He rode into cool, deep shadow, slid down from his saddle alongside stalls smelling of sweet hay where solid timber partitions offered some hope of shelter if it came to a gun battle . . . and Cramer reached out, traced the woodwork with his hand, let his thoughts look for solutions.

But of Jak La Roche and his horse there was no sign, and as weakness threatened to overcome him and Cramer sagged against his horse he felt the sharp pain as his blood-stiffened shirt pulled away from the wounds scarring his broad back, felt the strain in his injured leg and the trembling in both thighs that told him he was perilously close to the edge.

When he took a breath, clung to the saddle-horn and looked up, Padraig Flynn was walking through the barn doors accompanied by Frank Cooper and the lean cowhand. Both were toting shotguns. The three Blue Stack men were level, but spread out. Difficult targets, Cramer mused. But there's only one of them I want, so that's no problem — if I can stay on my feet.

'Draw faster, shoot straighter?' he said, mocking Frank Cooper's words, 'or just got hold of bigger guns?'

Cooper laughed. 'Either way's all the same,' he said.

'All right,' Cramer said to Flynn, 'let's hear this wasteful talk — then hand over my boy Johnny.'

Flynn shook his head. 'That can never be, and I'll tell — '

'Goddamn you!'

'Listen to me!' Flynn's chin jutted, his blue eyes became chips of ice in the dimness. 'So long ago that I've damn near forgot what it was like, we came over from Ireland, from a place much

218

like this close to the Blue Stack mountains in Donegal . . . ' He let that sink in as Cramer forced himself to breathe easy, to hang on and conserve his strength, to bide his time.

Flynn said, 'But if I have any remembrance at all then it tells me that this land is more cruel by far than the Emerald Isle, and so it took me by surprise when, after a couple of years of living rough, the good Lord blessed us — '

'You have the gall to speak of the Lord after — !'

'Blessed us with a little boy with hair like straw and . . . ' Flynn stopped, his voice clogged with emotion. Huskily, he said, 'He was two weeks old when he was taken by the Indians — '

'Farrall arranged that,' Cramer cut in, 'just as he arranged the replacement,' and he saw the muscles in Flynn's jaw whiten, heard the slow intake of breath, saw the man's stillness.

'For my wife, settling in this wild land was bad enough,' the Blue Stack boss continued softly. 'The loss of the boy was too much, and for a while . . . ' He shrugged. 'Maybe you're right about Farrall. Sure enough, when he brought . . . when he brought the boy in, yesterday, it was my wife he went to, as if he knew that once she held him . . . ' He spread his hands, while outside the barn the wind moaned and as straw rustled in a stall somewhere down the runway Cramer suddenly knew where La Roche had put his horse, and wondered about the little gambler.

'Our boy was lost to us when the Indians took him, because in no time at all they would change him out of all recognition, turn a gentle child into a spitting wildcat with a burning hatred of all people with pale faces . . . But now,' Padraig Flynn said, 'my wife truly believes she's got him back, and there's only one man who could spoil that — '

'And I will,' Cramer said tersely. 'It happens here, and it happens now, and I don't think you can take it. Because if the loss of a child sent your wife over the edge, what will she do when she loses her man?'

Straw rustled again as Frank Cooper shifted his feet. On the other side of Flynn the lean cowhand looked half asleep but, Cramer thought, was probably the most dangerous.

Padraig Flynn was frowning. Then he came to a decision and began to walk forward, his polished boots brushing through the loose straw. Cramer let his hand slip away from the saddle, tapped his horse on the rump and as it blew softly and moved off down the runway he stood swaying and his right hand drifted close to his tied-down holster.

Six feet away, Padraig Flynn stopped. He said, 'You're worried about shot-guns?' His eyebrows lifted. 'Here, catch.'

At another time, in another place, Joel Cramer would have let the shotgun fall and laughed in Flynn's face at his blatant trickery. But there was a distant singing in his brain, a creeping numbness in his limbs, and without thinking he took the thrown weapon in both hands, clutched the stock and smooth barrel as if to draw strength from the weapon's power.

'So now there's only two to bother you, and one six-gun,' Flynn said, 'and not a thing you can do about it,' and he swept back the tails of his coat and drew a Dragoon pistol, cocked it, levelled it at Cramer's forehead where the shine of sweat betrayed his weakness.

'A '73 Winchester suggests you're wrong,' Jak La Roche called.

The words fell like hard stones. Cooper and the lean cowhand swung round. Cramer looked past Flynn, saw the Louisiana gambler in the yard. Moonlight was pale on his face. The wind pushed him as he stood with his rifle high, at the aim.

'I guess,' Cramer told Flynn wearily, 'we've got ourselves a classic stand-off.'

'If one makes a play, both of us die? What the hell good is there in that?'

'None. That's why you're forced to back off, because I surely won't.'

The pistol in Flynn's hand was rock steady, the clear blue eyes unwavering. He said carefully, 'I give the word, two shotguns will cut your man to ribbons.'

'Those words leave your lips,' La Roche called, 'you're a dead man. Flynn.'

'So now it's three of us dead,' Flynn said, and for the first time his lips twisted in a wry smile. 'And when it's over, and the smoke has cleared, your boy . . . ' A softness came into his eyes; perhaps not that, Cramer thought, perhaps it was more the pain that comes when a man pleads for common sense with scant hope of success.

'When it's over,' Flynn said again, 'your boy will still be where he belongs.'

'Johnny? Where he belongs!'

'With his mother.'

'His mother's dead!'

'He doesn't know that.'

And Joel Cramer rocked on his heels, knocked backwards not by weakness,

223

but by words. Was this, then, common sense?

Nine months old, snatched from a damp dirt soddy in the dark night by unshaven men with scarred faces and eyes that glittered. Clutched in brawny arms, face pressed against rough clothing stinking of sweat. A pounding ride through wind and rain. And then . . .

Then comfort. Hot food. A warm, lamplit room. A woman's soft arms.

Sure, he'd remember his ma, miss her enough to shed hot tears. But in time — in an appallingly short time, because at nine months the days come and go and to a child there is the present and the future but very little past — in time, he would forget.

Face it, Cramer told himself, his thoughts bleak: there's no way out of this. The law could maybe handle it — but Farrall was law. But if you can't replace Johnny's ma — because maybe, in the kid's mind the replacement was already being met with shy affection

— you sure as hell can make sure he's always got his pa. Not close, maybe. Maybe not even so he knows he's there . . .

'What's the deal?' he said hoarsely.

'Work for me.' The pistol stayed in place. The blue eyes were watchful. 'I'll shortly be hiring for the spring round-ups. You'll be part of the crew, but always out of sight of the house — '

'No.' Cramer shook his head, saw Padraig Flynn's lips tighten, the sudden hardening of those eyes.

'I think what Tucson's got in mind,' La Roche said, his way still barred by the two cowhands, 'is a place called Pueblo.'

'The soddy was part way there,' Cramer said, following La Roche's lead, feeling a sudden strength flowing into the vacuum left by the uncertainty of the past hours. 'My aim was to raise cattle and, hell, me and my pard can make a damn sight better job of it at Pueblo than Dyke Manson.' He looked across at La Roche, caught the

Louisiana gambler's covert wink, looked questioningly at Flynn.

'Done. The boy will be looked after. I'll sign over Pueblo. Now, that's my side of the bargain, so . . . '

The Dragoon's hammer was eased down, the pistol lowered. Already Cooper and the lean gunman had turned and were walking away.

'We'll use your barn for the night, be on our way at dawn,' Cramer said, and saw Flynn nod his agreement and pouch the pistol, still patiently waiting.

'My side of it?' Cramer eased his shoulders, said softly. 'I'll keep out of the way, work that spread, see Johnny from time to time, from a distance. It'll be enough, just. But . . . ' He pursed his lips, feeling the sour taste in his mouth left by those words, looked wonderingly down the tricky road they were contemplating and said, 'This is the right decision, for now, but what I can't do is say clear what'll happen when the boy reaches fifteen, sixteen. Maybe then, if it's put to him — '

'We'll deal with that when the time comes.'

Flynn hesitated, seemed to contemplate shaking hands with Cramer, then decided against it, nodded curtly and turned on his heel. He was approaching the steps to the house when La Roche entered the barn; his dark figure was outlined in the light flooding from the open front door as the woman appeared, still carrying Johnny Cramer.

They went inside the house. The door closed. There was a finality about the click of the latch, and when Cramer turned away there was a look in his eyes that was not lost on La Roche.

'Not the best of finishes,' he said quietly, 'but better than a bloodbath.'

'What I thought,' Joel Cramer said. He began unbuttoning buttons, said to La Roche, 'How's it feel to be in the cattle business, pard?'

'I like the sound of pard, better'n cattle,' La Roche said, grinning, 'but I'll get used to it. He watched Cramer strip off the bloodstained shirt and roll it

227

into a ball, said, 'You aimin' to wash that, or burn it?'

'Neither,' said Tucson Joel Cramer. 'I reckon I'll keep it for fifteen years . . . just in case I start forgettin', as time passes, that the boy in that house is my son — mine, and Fran's — and always will be.'

He crossed to his horse, stuffed the filthy shirt into his saddle bag and began untying his blanket roll.

THE END

GUNS OF THE GAMBLER

M. Duggan

Destitute gambler Ben Crow arrives in Mallory keen to claim his inheritance, only to discover that rancher Edward Bacon has other ideas. Set up by Miss Dorothy, who had fooled him completely, Ben finds himself dangling on the end of a rope. Saved from death, Ben sets off in pursuit of Miss Dorothy, determined upon retribution. However, his quest for vengeance turns into a rescue mission when she is kidnapped by a crazy man-burning bandit.

SIDEWINDER

John Dyson

All Flynn wants is to be Marshal of Tucson, but he is framed by the territory's richest rancher, Frank Buchanan, and thrown into Yuma prison. Five years later Flynn comes out, intent on clearing his name and burning for vengeance. Fists thud, knives flash and bullets fly as he rides both sides of the law and participates in kidnapping and double-dealing. He is once again arrested for a murder of which he is innocent. Can he escape the noose a second time?

THE BLOODING OF JETHRO

Frank Fields

When Jethro Smith's family is murdered by outlaws, vengeance is the one thing on his mind. He meets the brother of one of the murderers, who attempts to exploit Jethro's grudge in the pursuit of his own vendetta. The local preacher, formerly a sheriff, teaches Jethro how to use a gun. With his new-found skills, Jethro and his somewhat unwelcome friend pit themselves against seemingly impossible odds. Whatever the outcome lead would surely fly.

SEVEN HELLS AND A SIXGUN

Jack Greer

Jim Cayman had been warned about Daphne Rankin, his boss's wife, and her little ways. When Daphne made a play for Jim and he resisted, the result was painful and about what he had feared. But suddenly matters went beyond the expected and he found himself left to die an awful death. Only then did he realise that there was far more than a woman scorned. He vowed that if he could escape from the hell-hole he would surely solve the mystery — and settle some scores.